W9-AYP-574

AN AVALON HISTORICAL ROMANCE

A Morgan Brothers Romance

A WANTED MAN
Nancy J. Parra

Brianna McGraw ventures out West to find and rescue her brother from bandits who will sell him illegally to the highest bidder. Separated after they were orphaned a few years ago, Brianna has worked hard as a librarian to save money for the trip. But when she arrives, she realizes she has to somehow come up with a thousand dollars to buy him back.

She then sees a wanted poster with a sufficient reward and decides to become a bounty hunter, accomplishing two good deeds at once—bringing a criminal to justice and saving her brother.

Trey Morgan's renegade days are long over. He is at home on his ranch, tending to his cattle, when Brianna appears and arrests him. He is more amused than concerned, wondering how she thinks she's going to drag him 900 miles through the mountains.

To his surprise, Brianna proves over and over again that she is intelligent and strong enough to make the long and grueling trip. While he quietly observes his beautiful captor, his discomfort grows when she begins to win more and more of his respect and admiration.

Soon, the threat his beautiful captor holds over him is not so much in the pistol she wields, but the lasso she has firmly fastened over his heart.

A WANTED MAN

•

Nancy J. Parra

AVALON BOOKS
NEW YORK

PRINTED IN THE UNITED STATES OF AMERICA
ON ACID-FREE PAPER
BY HADDON CRAFTSMEN, BLOOMSBURG, PENNSYLVANIA

For my dear friends, Candy Cole, Sharon Flannery,
De Ann Sicard and Gay Thornton,
thanks for years of laughter, tears, encouragement and comfort.
I couldn't have done it without you.

49101

Prologue

"The boy is mine, bought and paid for fair an' square."

Brianna McGraw narrowed her eyes at the words of the pockmarked man who held her brother. Arguing with the old miner was not having any effect. His brains had turned to mush years ago under this dreadful Nevada sun. "Then I will buy him back."

"You ain't got enough money," the second man at the table said. A wicked gleam filled his eyes and Brianna tightened the hold on her parasol. She was not above defending herself.

"Name your price and we'll see if I can pay it or not."

The first man pulled her brother closer. "Well, now, we've gotten pretty attached to the boy since he came off'n that there train, ain't that right, Melvin."

"Yep," the second man said, then spit. The glob

1

landed near her feet. Although disgusted, Brianna ignored the action. She had to ignore it, as she ignored everything else in this filthy building that passed for a saloon. The dying Nevada mining town stood on the border of hell. At least, it was hot enough to be a level in Dante's hell.

But this hell was the miners' home. Therefore, they had the advantage. If she were to save her brother, she would have to sacrifice her own sensibilities.

"How much?" she pressed.

"How much you figure, Melvin? Fifty? A hunnerd?"

"One thousand," Melvin said and then grinned slow. "This here boy's worth one thousand American dollars to us, ain't that right, Zeke?"

"One thousand dollars!" She gasped.

"An' don't think you can go to the sheriff neither, missy," Zeke said. "He'll as likely arrest you as us. It's against the law to try to buy these here boys. I'll be sure to tell him you made the first offer an' I have a whole saloon full of witnesses. Old Jeb will haul you away in handcuffs."

Alarm shivered down her back. Justice at the orphanage had been swift and inequitable. It had left Bri with the sure and certain knowledge that the only person who could help her was herself. "I won't go to the sheriff, but I don't have a thousand dollars on me."

"See, I told ya, ya couldn't pay. Not unless ya got yerself a silver mine." Zeke squinted at her from beneath his sweat and dust–coated hat. "Ya ain't got one of those, has ya?"

"I most certainly have not," she said and opened her

purse. She reached inside and pulled out her change purse. "I'll give you two hundred dollars for the boy right now. Cash." She withdrew a wad of money and the room became silent. She had the feeling every pair of eyes in the room was on the bundle in her hand; even the rats under the floorboards. A bead of sweat trickled down her back. She may have just made a terrible tactical error.

Brianna did not look around. Now was not the time to show fear. This pack of wild men would be upon her in an instant and all would be lost. She turned a lazy gaze upon the two who had her brother, then placed the money on the table. "All you have to do is hand over the boy."

There was a long moment of silence, and then Zeke reached for the money. Melvin stabbed his knife through it before Zeke could grab it. Then he turned his beady blue gaze on her. "It ain't enough."

"It's all I have."

"Not all." He grinned at her and her stomach lurched. "We'll trade ya the boy for the two hunnerd and one hunnerd days of your services. Just for Zeke an' myself, of course."

"No!" Ethan shouted.

Brianna looked at her twelve-year-old brother. He was thinner than she remembered and signs of beatings marred his cheeks and his arms. She vowed then and there to see these men brought down, and if she were going to do that, then she would have to be free. To be free, she would have to be strong.

She reached out and snagged the knife from the bills

and pointed it against Melvin's adam's apple. "No deal."

He didn't dare swallow or the knife would cut his throat.

"Then the price is still one thousand dollars," Zeke said. "Ain't that right, Melvin?"

Brianna's gaze never left his. If this was a game of chicken, she would not be the first to crack.

"One thousand," Melvin croaked out between dried lips. Brianna pressed the knife closer.

"You can have my boy for that there two hunnerd," someone called out. "He's bigger than their boy. Able to put in a full day's work."

Brianna let her gaze roam from man to man in the room. "How many of you have boys off that train?"

"Heck, if you're offerin' two hunnerd, we all got boys off that train," a third man called out.

"How many?" she demanded.

The room fell silent. She turned her attention back to Melvin and pressed the knife in until a slow trickle of blood dulled the surface. "Seven," he croaked.

"Fifteen," someone hollered from the back.

She looked back at the men in the room. It was then that she spotted it. The wanted poster. The one that offered a thousand–dollar reward for a man, if you brought him in alive. Brianna's mind formed a fast and clear plan.

If she brought in the villain, she could get the money without the sheriff ever needing to know why. She reached over and stuffed the wad of money back into her purse, then slowly took the knife from Melvin's throat.

"I'll be back at the next full moon," she declared. "With one thousand dollars in my hand. It will go for the best-tended boy in this saloon."

"Hey," Zeke whined. "That was our price."

"It seems I got a better offer." She jerked her head toward the side of the room. "He says his boy is stronger and it looks to me like you haven't fed this one in a week. I will have that thousand, and when I do, I'll pick the strongest, healthiest boy."

"That ain't fair."

She glanced at her brother, then back at Zeke. "You have one month to fatten yours up. I suggest you get started."

That said, she tucked the knife into the waistband of her skirt and raised her chin. "Good day, gentlemen." She picked up her skirt and made a beeline for the entrance, stopping only long enough to tear the wanted poster off the wall.

Chapter One

Trouble snaked its way across Trey Morgan's land. It was the worst kind of trouble as far as Trey was concerned.

It was a lone woman on horseback.

Trey watched her double back twice before settling in a nearby grove of trees. Who was she? What was she doing on his land?

He'd been out checking the fences when he first saw a flash of sunlight come from the side of his mountain. So he'd found a vantage spot and watched her sneak through his land like a renegade Indian, quiet and determined.

It was hot and dry. The grass crunched beneath his horse, yet she managed to not make a sound. The only thing to reach his keen ears was the constant lazy hum of summer insects.

He dismounted, left his horse to free range, and eased in for a closer look.

She was dressed to blend into her surroundings. The dark wool of her split skirt was the color of the tree trunks. Her long-sleeved jacket was deep green. A brown Stetson covered her head, and her brunet hair was plaited into one long braid that trailed down her back.

She was also well armed with what looked like a Colt in a holster hanging against her shapely hip. She wore it like she knew how to use it.

The overall picture gave her the look of someone with something to hide. His curiosity deepened when her hands, covered by brown leather gloves, tugged a spyglass out of her saddlebags. Opening it, she studied the trail behind her.

Trey frowned. Was someone following her? He scanned the horizon. No one was in sight. Glancing back, he watched her dismount in one smooth movement. She must feel safe, which meant she had no idea he watched her.

Even more curious was the big painted mare she had tied to her saddle. Who was it for? The horse was completely saddled yet riderless. Trey looked around again. Was she meeting someone? If so, then who? Or, was she hiding from someone? Again he wondered who and, more important, why on his land?

He didn't like questions. Didn't care for devious women either. It irritated him that this one had interrupted his day.

He watched as she put the glass away, took a swig from her canteen, and contemplated a piece of paper as if it were a treasure map. He scowled as he came to a clear and immediate conclusion.

She was a thief.

She had stolen a map to some poor miner's claim, then hightailed it out of town. He could add claim jumper to her list of sins as well for it was certain she would convince everyone the claim belonged to her dear departed father.

She turned her head enough that he could make out her profile. It stopped him in his tracks.

Her skin, flushed from the heat, was fair pink along an alabaster cheek. He saw her high forehead edged with dark winged brows and a straight nose, lush eyelashes, and parted lips. It was the mouth that got to him.

He'd thought that after Katherine he was immune to women's charms. Katherine, the conniving witch, had taught him a valuable lesson. Women were out for only one thing—money—and they'd do anything to get it, even kill their unborn child. It was a hard-learned lesson. One he thought he *had* learned.

It annoyed him to find out he wasn't immune after all.

This woman, whoever she was, made his gut react in a way he hadn't felt since he was seventeen and kissed Jenny Perkins full on the lips.

He ground his teeth in frustration. He didn't want this reaction. If he knew women, and he did, this one had used her charms on some poor sucker until she got his treasure. She probably stole the guy's horse and saddle too, just so he couldn't follow her.

The thought left a bitter taste in Trey's mouth. Well, now she was on his land, and he'd see she didn't get very far.

Wyoming was hotter than Brianna expected. From what she had read, the average July temperature would have accommodated her current outfit. Today was definitely not average.

Her guise was perfect for hiding in the mountains, perfect for sneaking through enemy territory, but at the moment terribly uncomfortable.

She wiped the sweat from her forehead and was glad that she had chosen not to put on the recommended but scratchy wool underclothes. Her thin cotton bloomers and shift might not be wise, but they were comfortable.

She sipped tin-tasting water from her canteen and took one last long look at the wanted poster. She had the criminal's face memorized. It was a visage to frighten little children into going straight to bed at night.

He had a strong brow ridge leading to a classic nose and firm, almost sensuous, mouth. She pursed her lips. It would have been a handsome face really except for the eyes. Those eyes were completely devoid of emotion.

It left her cold even in the heat of July.

It was clear that Robert Angus Morgan, the third,

alias Trey Morgan, did not care whether he lived or died. That was what made him so dangerous.

She drew in a deep breath and gathered her courage. This was not going to be easy. She knew it and was prepared. After all, she had read *The Complete Guide to Bounty Hunting* by Wilford Bench and poured over Mr. Albert Fry's *Guide to All Things Western* and then his follow-up, *Backtracking and Other Indian Tricks*.

She might be a young greenhorn from Boston, but she was nothing if not a quick learner. For the first time in her life her librarian skills had come in handy. First in tracking down her brother and now in finding Morgan. She was certain they would be enough to take her through the wilderness.

She glanced at the villain's picture. He was clearly a clever, cold-hearted adversary.

It didn't matter. All that mattered to her was that she get her reward and rescue those poor boys.

To do that she would simply have to be cleverer.

There was no sound, no whisper to warn her—but she felt a brush of air along her skin and whirled. Her six-shooter slid easily into her hand. A woman alone had to know how to protect herself, and Bri had been shooting for years now.

Heart racing, eyes wary, she faced the menace. It took all of her resolve not to stumble back against her horse. He was bigger than most men were. His dark hair hung in braids beneath the felt hat that shielded his eyes. There was something familiar about him. His nose was straight and true, his jaw strong, his chin held the faintest dimple. She felt her mouth go dry.

He exuded power and grace, and she dared not blink for fear he would move quickly and deadly in that instant. "My gun is loaded and I know how to use it." She kept the words even and fierce. In reality, fear kept her rooted to the spot.

There was a long moment of heart-stopping silence. He eyed her from under his brim. His arms crossed across his chest. She felt every hair on the back of her neck rise.

The gun in her hand did not waiver. It seemed they were at a stalemate, each waiting for the other to blink first. No man had ever challenged her like this. She found it . . . interesting.

Finally he stepped toward her, silent, steady, and dangerous. She held her ground and her gun aimed right for his heart. "Close enough."

He paused and pushed his hat up and away from his eyes. It was then that her blood ran cold and the gun slipped ever so slightly.

It was the man in the wanted poster, Trey Morgan.

The very man she had come to collect.

"You recognized me," he said. "Why?" His voice skittered along her nerves. It was rich and deep and promising. Oddly, she was attracted to the sound. But now was not the time to ponder her strange reaction; lives hung in the balance. She steeled herself for the moments to come.

"I saw the wanted poster," she replied. It wasn't what she had imagined she would say when she found him.

No, she had imagined herself calling his name.

She'd imagined being on horseback and therefore at a height advantage. She'd imagined the click of the hammer as she drew it back and the relief when he gave in.

Now, face to face with the man, she realized two things. One, *he* was looking down at *her* and, two, he would not come easily.

"Which?"

The word bothered her more than she wanted to admit. This man who stood in front of her accepted the fact that he was a wanted man. He didn't want to know how or why. No, he wanted to know *which*. That meant there was probably more than one wanted poster.

Sweat ran down her back, tickling her. She told herself it was from the heat, not fear.

"Durango, Nevada," she replied. "I'm taking you back."

Most men would have grinned at her bravado. She'd been prepared for that. But not this man; he simply leveled his head and stared her down. Bri felt that stare clear to her toes.

Time to change tactics. She blinked slowly, insolently, then drew back the hammer of her gun. The click that locked it in place was the loudest thing in the air, second only to the silence that sizzled around them.

"Throw down your guns and the Bowie knife."

His eyes narrowed then. "Why?"

"I told you. I'm taking you in, and I promise you, I can and will kill you here if I have to, and drag your dead body back to Durango." She kept her aim steady and true as she lifted one shoulder in a half shrug. "It matters not to me."

"It's a long way to go with a dead man," he said. "The stink would be so bad the wolves would follow you through the mountains."

She lifted a corner of her mouth in a fair imitation of a grin and tilted her head. "I'm not afraid of a few wolves. Your choice. Throw down your weapons or die."

He waited four heartbeats, then reached for his guns. "Easy," she commanded. Her mouth was suddenly dry as a desert. He threw both guns at her feet, then reached for the Bowie. His eyes glinted as a thought occurred to him. "Don't even think about it," she said. "I'm a good shot. I'd have both the knife and you."

He removed it using only two fingers and in one fluid motion tossed it. The huge knife landed hilt up in the dirt at her feet. She congratulated herself on not flinching. His gaze met hers. "Anything else?"

"Take off your boots."

For a moment he looked like he was going to balk. She pointed her gun at his feet. "I suppose I could wing you instead."

He muttered something under his breath and removed his boots.

"Toss them here." They landed with a thud exactly where she pointed. "Thank you."

"You're welcome," he replied. His tone mocked

her. She refused to bite. It was a long way to Nevada and she couldn't let him get to her.

She reached over and snatched handcuffs off her saddle. "Turn around."

He raised an eyebrow.

She frowned. "I said turn around."

He turned maddeningly slow. She stepped within arm's reach. Each step made her more aware of the size of him. He was a head taller than she was and his shoulders were broad enough to block her view. He smelled oddly compelling, like good soap and honest hard work. Hardly what she expected from a killer.

"Put your hands behind your back."

He did as she asked. His hands were rough and callused. Small nicks and cuts slashed through his skin. "What have you been doing?" she asked, tempted to soothe the tiny cuts.

"Repairing barbed–wire fences," he said.

She got a hold of herself. The man was not to be pitied. He was a killer. "Didn't your mama tell you that you should wear gloves?"

"My Ma's dead."

"Oh. Well." She felt like an idiot for bringing up the subject and reminded herself yet again that he was a killer. "That would certainly explain your behavior." She swallowed her emotion, stepped in closer, and shoved her gun barrel in his back. "Don't get any ideas. I don't trust you farther than I can throw you and that's not very far."

She put the cuffs around his wrists and tightened

them, and then she stepped back. "That should keep you for the moment."

He lazily turned around. The smoothness of the motion did not escape her. He was not afraid of her or the handcuffs. She narrowed her gaze. It struck her then he could probably get out of them. She had no idea how, but he didn't seem too worried. It was as if he didn't believe she would take him. As if he thought it was some sort of a joke. That really irked her. How dare he not believe she was serious?

Well, he would have to believe she was serious when they arrived in Durango—and she was going to make sure they arrived in Durango. Her brother was counting on her.

"Where's your horse?" she asked.

"At the top of the ridge."

"Is he hobbled or tied?"

"I left him to range."

That was good news. She could safely leave the animal. It would find its way home. But that also meant she had little time. From what she had heard, the Morgan brothers were a close gang and very good trackers. She'd have to disappear with this hulking man before the sun set and the horse found its way back home.

Bri released the hammer on her gun and shoved it in the holster she wore on her hip. Then she grabbed a length of rough rope off her saddle and moved toward the big man. She stopped a yard away. The distance did little to diminish his size or the power he exuded. "Turn back around."

He glared at her. She ignored him. "Turn," she ordered. With a sigh she put her hand on the butt of her gun. He did as she said, and she slung the rope between his cuffed hands. Careful to stay a safe distance away, she tied it to a nearby tree. He stood there in his stockings looking for all the world as if he were bored.

"I take it this isn't the first time you've been captured."

He answered with a huge yawn.

"Of course not," she muttered. "Well, it will be your last." Again he didn't seem too impressed. She kept him in her peripheral vision as she picked up his weapons. She unloaded them, tucking the bullets into the small pocket she had sewn in her waistband. Then she packed the guns into her saddlebag.

She picked up the Bowie knife. It was, cool, smooth, and carefully honed. She contemplated tossing it into the brush, but the knife was too beautiful to throw away. "Throw me the scabbard."

"Why?"

"I've decided to keep the knife."

"I can't reach it." He held up his cuffed hands. The scabbard was tied to his belt.

She frowned. If she wanted it, she would have to get close to him. Very close. "Never mind."

He shrugged. "Up to you."

She opened her saddlebag and pulled out a small bag of flour. Then she untied the top and plunged the knife inside.

"Hey!"

"It won't harm it." She closed the bag over the knife handle and tied it closed.

"It's a weapon, not a cooking utensil," he sneered.

"Indeed," she said, and pulled her own knife out of the scabbard that hung from her belt. "You're not the only one who knows something about knives."

Her friends at Mrs. Persimmon's boardinghouse in Boston had insisted that she be handy with more than a gun before she headed out to the wilds of the west in search of her brother. Right now she was very grateful for their advice.

She turned to the man who was the key to saving her brother. He leaned against the tree, his massive body looking relaxed, but beneath the pose he radiated a coiled energy. Taking him had been easier than she dreamed. Keeping him was going to be the real problem.

Bri knew beyond a shadow of a doubt she had a real tiger by the tail. She simply had to be swifter and smarter than he if she was going to make it all the way to Nevada alive.

"Before you get too sure of yourself, I believe there is something you should know about me," she said as she slid her small knife into position. She let it fly with one swift flick of her wrist. He did not flinch as the knife dug into the bark of the tree a half an inch from his ear. "I'm not afraid to fight dirty."

He raised an eyebrow but didn't respond.

"Just so long as you know," she said. "Then you can't say I didn't warn you." She untied the rope and

Nancy J. Parra

pulled him toward her horses. "We'll take my horses—"

"Might as well take mine," he said. "He'll follow us if you don't."

"I don't believe you," she said. "You'll take the paint." She tied the rope around the paint's saddle horn. "You'll have to figure out yourself how to mount her."

"Mounting has never been a problem," he drawled.

She narrowed her eyes at his insolence. "A gentleman would never speak to a lady like that."

"I'm no gentleman," he said. "I'm a Morgan."

"Well, gentleman or not, watch your mouth or I'll gag it." It made her mad that he thought he could speak to her like that. If it had been Boston, she would have slapped his face. "Get on."

She stormed over and retrieved her knife from the tree. This wasn't Boston and he wasn't a gentleman. He was a killer. She could never forget that.

She watched his movement from the corner of her eye. He simply put his right foot in the stirrup and swung his left up and over. The movement was graceful and bore out what must have been a lifetime of ease in the saddle.

She swallowed her astonishment and climbed up on her own horse. "We have a lot of miles to cover and not much time," she explained. "Let me know if you need a break."

He made a noise that sounded like a snort.

She ignored him and pulled her horse's reins until he started up the top of the ridge. The paint's reins were tied to the back of her saddle. Both animals were completely under her control.

They rode out of the shade of the small clump of trees and she glanced at the sun. It was around three in the afternoon. She had little time to double back and cover her tracks before dark. Little time to follow the advice she had learned from Mr. Fry's *Guide to All Things Western* and disappear into the landscape.

Chapter Two

Trey had a long, long time to contemplate the situation he'd gotten himself into. His arms ached from the awkward position she tied them in. It was a smart move, really, one that had surprised him.

Heck, everything about her surprised him. He knew the moment she recognized him. For some reason, he was abnormally aware of her tiniest movements—the way her eyelashes fluttered, the small sharp inhalation of breath between her lips.

He hadn't believed her when she told him she'd come for him. She looked too darn soft to be a bounty hunter. A real criminal would chew her up and spit her out.

He'd been wrong, though. She didn't back down from his glare, a look which had been perfected to make even the bravest of men get weak in the knees. Instead she'd stared him down. It was a heady feeling.

The steely determination in her forest–green eyes had told him she would shoot him. It peaked his interest all right. His mind had wandered over what other kinds of things she might also be determined to do.

He shook the stupid thoughts from his head. Years ago, he'd sworn not to get involved with a woman ever again. It was an oath he couldn't let time and female wiles erode. So, if it wasn't stupidity that got him in this situation, what was it?

Curiosity. That's what it was. He was curious about her.

She'd proved smart, too smart. He'd watched in admiration as she covered their tracks in a near flawless manner. But he wasn't worried she'd get him all the way to Nevada. Matt and Tag could track bug prints on granite. His brothers would come for him.

That's what worried him. How was he going to explain to them his shoeless feet and useless hands? They wouldn't believe this mere chit of a girl did this to him. But what they really wouldn't believe is that he'd let her.

He blew out a deep breath. No, his brothers were never going to let him live this one down.

She rode like a demon on a mission, accomplishing more in half a day than most did in a full day. Her choice of horses was flawless. He recognized the paint he rode along with the black she led with. They were both his brother Tag's horses, bred to withstand the complexities of mountain travel. She'd picked solid trail horses.

He wondered who helped her. Then he wondered how she got that help. He might be curious about her, heck he might even be attracted to her, but that didn't mean he trusted her.

Two hours into darkness, she finally stopped. "We'll camp here." She eyed him. "I suppose you're going to need help dismounting."

He merely looked at her. He could fall off the horse, of course, or for that matter probably kick himself free, but his arms were constrained and it might be awkward. Besides, he wondered what she would do about it.

She dismounted. Her movements were stiff from the riding, but she didn't make a sound of complaint. "I'll help you," she said resignedly. "But I've still got my knife, so don't think about trying anything foolish."

Oh, he wanted to try something foolish all right. That was the problem. Like it or not he wanted to kiss her.

"Curiosity killed the stupid cat," he muttered under his breath.

"What?"

"Nothing."

"Well, do you want my help or not?"

"I could fall off."

"You might get your foot caught in the stirrup. Then I wouldn't blame your horse if she were to get spooked and drag you to Nevada. Is that what you want?"

"No, ma'am."

"Then let me think." She stood for a moment and

looked up at him as if contemplating a puzzle. "Okay." Absently she chewed on her lower lip. The motion was highly distracting. "Think you could swing your leg over?"

He blinked and had to think through her words. Of course he could. He leaned into the stirrup near her and swung the opposite leg over in an easy stretch.

The glint of admiration in her eye did a lot to soothe his bruised ego. Heck, he'd lived most of his life on a horse. Tricks like this were learned at an early age to impress his younger brothers.

"Great. Now I'll unhook the stirrup from your foot and you can just jump down." She took a step closer and rested her darned pig-sticker knife along the back of his knee. "Don't try anything."

Irritated, he didn't even give her the satisfaction of a reply. She slipped the stirrup off his toe and tucked it into the side of the saddle. Then she stepped away. "You're on your own."

She didn't wait to watch him dismount. Instead she turned her attention to her horse. He slid down with ease and stretched his shoulders from side to side. Darn. He was stiffer than he'd ever been his entire life.

"There's a couple of trees over there if you need to . . . you know."

He raised one eyebrow at her. "And just exactly how do you propose I do that? My hands are cuffed behind my back."

She flushed. He couldn't see it too well in the dark, but he swore the heat rolled off of her. "I'm not helping you with that," she stated briskly and turned her back on him. "You'll have to wait until the horses are cared for and I'm prepared to cut you free."

She went to work on her horse.

He grinned into the darkness. Even embarrassed she held her own. He leaned against a nearby boulder and waited. She was a piece of work. "You're a hard woman," he said out loud.

She paused for a moment, then pulled her saddle off. "I don't think I've ever been described as that," she said, her voice soft in the quiet of the mountain night. "I suppose if I was in your position, I'd think that too." She tossed the saddle to the ground and looked at him. "But I'm not. If I were truly hard, I would have killed you the moment I recognized you."

"But you didn't," he pointed out.

She turned back to her horse and rubbed it down. "No, I didn't. I just pray to the good Lord that I didn't make a mistake."

He shifted against the weathered stone and watched her. She did a thorough job of rubbing down her animal and checking its hooves before hobbling it for the night. "So, tell me," he had to ask, "why didn't you?"

"Maybe I didn't want to deal with the wolves."

"You said you weren't afraid of wolves."

She stopped just out of reach. "You're right, I did say that. Must be the stench then. I always did prefer things that smelled nice."

He thought about how good she smelled earlier when she'd leaned in close to offer him water. She'd smelled like peppermint. That was a contradiction in itself. Bounty hunters never smelled like candy.

"I suppose you expect me to uncuff you now," she said with a sigh.

"It's not for me. It's for the horse." He pointed out the rope that still tied the cuffs to his saddle.

"Of course," she replied. "And don't think about overpowering me. I still have my knife and yours."

He watched her untie the rope from the saddle horn. It slid to the ground and freed the tension from his hands.

"Turn around."

He did what she asked. He was aware of her behind him. Of the scent of her skin as the wind blew from her to him. The heat that rolled off her in the cold of a mountain night.

He heard the key turn in the cuffs and then the metal fell away from his wrists. He rubbed them and turned. She was already well out of reach with a cocked and loaded pistol in her hand.

She nodded toward the two closest trees. "I can hear your every move, so—"

"I know, I know," he grumbled. "Don't try anything." That said, he moved toward the darkness. He didn't want to try anything. She intrigued him. He had to know what drove a woman like her to bounty hunt. Heck, with her looks she'd have been able to capture any number of rich and powerful men. She should be sitting in some mansion in Denver right now with her feet up and servants waiting on her every demand.

But she wasn't. Why?

Katherine had moved on to the next richest man, discarding Trey and his child like so much waste. The experience had left him bitter and angry, until time wore away the anger, leaving only bitterness. Trey figured all women were after one thing, and it wasn't love.

But then again, there was his brother's new wife. She was different. She was . . . crazy. He allowed a smile to touch the edge of his mouth. No, that wasn't right. She drove his brother crazy; yes, that was more accurate.

He blew out a long breath. This woman was about to drive him crazy. Him, bitter Trey Morgan. Why? That was the big question. He needed to know why he wanted to kiss her. After all he'd been through, he had to figure out what made him want a crazy, pushy, desperate woman. Because that was the only thing he was certain about her. She was desperate.

Why else would she think she could drag a big man like him nine hundred miles through the wilderness alone. She was either desperate or crazier than a loon.

At this moment, he felt he had to know which it was. With any luck, he'd get it out of her before his brothers showed up. In the meantime it was best to wait and pay attention to the things she didn't say.

A million thoughts crowded her tired mind as she heard him wander off a few yards. She ached so bad from being on horseback all day it made her wonder at her own sanity. She told herself to buck up. It would get better as she closed the miles between her and her little brother. Her plan was not a bad one, just harder than she'd ever dreamed it would be. She took a deep breath and stretched.

Adventures and quests were so captivating in books. The stories had left her breathless and daydreaming. Reality was different. She was cold and sore and hungry and she knew beyond a shadow of a doubt she'd be pushed beyond her endurance by the time they reached Nevada. It didn't help either that she was attracted to the killer she'd captured. The man was a handsome devil.

It was the devil part she had to remember. If she forgot that, she'd be in worse trouble than her brother. The killer finished and strode toward her. "No fire tonight," she said and stifled a yawn. "We've only got a few hours to rest and it's not worth it."

"What's your hurry?"

She didn't reply. Instead she jerked the six-shooter toward the pile the saddles made on the ground. "Make yourself comfortable, Mr. Morgan."

He sauntered over and slung his body down so that he could lean against his saddle. "You ever say anything that's not an order? You sound like a darn schoolteacher." His hat hid his eyes from her. She couldn't tell what he meant by that. So, she ignored him and coiled the length of rope in her hand.

She stepped in closer and hunkered down in front of him. "I'm not a teacher," she said as she tied the rope around his feet. "Hold out your hands."

"Yes, ma'am." The words were insolent but he held

out his hands. She sighed. She did sound mean and bossy. It didn't matter. What mattered was getting him back to Durango so she could rescue her brother. She cuffed him and then slid the rope around the cuffs connecting his hands and his feet.

The rope was a yard or so long. It meant he'd have to sit slightly bent, but it was the best she could do barring shooting him and putting both of them out of their misery.

She got up, uncocked the gun, and put it back in its holster. "Hungry?"

"More than you'd know," he replied.

Guilt shot through her. He'd been out working the fences when she found him. He'd probably not eaten since breakfast, and she'd not stopped long enough to eat.

"I've got biscuits and jerky." She turned back and rummaged through her supplies. "When we make it into Colorado, I've got flour and such for biscuits." She grabbed their canteens and moved back beside him. "I'm a good enough shot to get us some fresh meat, but for now, this will have to do." She sat down beside him and offered him a tilted canteen.

He opened his mouth and drank. Then she took a hunk of jerky and offered it to him. He bent down and she felt the slight brush of his hair along her wrist as he bit off a portion and straightened to chew.

They ate in silence. His dark gaze watched her like a hawk watches its prey. She was too tired to worry about what he thought. Her own thoughts wandered to the small feather bed she usually slept in. It was tucked away in a cozy attic room in the boardinghouse in Boston where she lived. It had been her home since she was sixteen and able to leave the orphanage and get a job at the library. It had been her home while she put herself through college. All that seemed a world away. She wondered briefly: if she closed her eyes, when she opened them again would this all be a dream?

She shook away the silly thought and took a long drink of the water. She'd refill the canteens at the stream in the morning, but right now she needed to rest. "Water?"

"Sure." He opened his mouth and she lifted the canteen. Water chugged out at an alarming rate, splashing him completely.

Horrified, she jumped up. "I'm sorry. I didn't mean to drown you."

He spat and sputtered, trying to catch his breath. She took the cotton kerchief from around her neck and leaned down to wipe his face.

"I'm so sorry." She wiped his face as she would her younger brother's; but this man was not her brother. In fact he was such a large man that she had to practically sit in his lap to get to his face. She hadn't thought, she'd merely leaped to his rescue.

Now they were a breath apart. He still smelled good, like horse and man and something else, something she couldn't put her finger on. His eyes glittered in the starlight. His long lashes clumped with drops of water. A droplet ran from his forehead down along his high cheek to the dark stubble on his rock hard jaw.

She had the strong urge to kiss it away.

Chapter Three

The impulse was insane. Her gaze moved to the lush depth of his mouth. It looked firm but not hard, and she wondered what it might taste like. He inhaled sharply.

She realized then that she was too close and staring like a lovesick cow. For goodness sake the man was a wanted killer. "Sorry," she said. The word came out hoarse as if she'd just woken up. She jumped up and strode away hoping she could cover the awkward situation by checking on the horses.

The brisk walk was exactly what she needed. What she wanted to do was kick herself, but she was too tired. It had been a hard and rocky climb. The doubling back had taken a great deal of concentration and her head ached from thinking.

As they had climbed into the mountains, the air had turned cool to the point of cold. She knew it had something to do with the altitude. It was said people reacted differently to altitude. Maybe that was what this was all about. Maybe she was simply tired and light-headed from the thin air.

The man was a wanted killer. He must have killed many, ruthlessly, to have a thousand-dollar reward. Maybe he even made a hobby out of raping women and murdering children. She shivered.

That's it. Think clear. The man's a killer. Except his eyes didn't have the look of a killer. No, even though she'd trussed him up like a thanksgiving turkey, he still watched with curiosity, concern, and something else. Something that stroked her ego and made her feel . . . pretty.

She reached her horse and petted it. The animal felt warm, its hair rough to the touch. She imagined her captive's stubble face would feel close to the same. "Get a grip, McGraw," she said to the night sky. She didn't need to feel pretty. What she needed was to rescue her brother. "Get some rest," she ordered herself. "Things will definitely look different in the morning."

She patted the horse and checked its hobble. It wouldn't go very far. She checked the paint. It, too, was simply grazing and enjoying the rest. "Good girls. Rest. Tomorrow we ride hard, but I promise only for a few days." She kissed the horse's nose. "Just enough to get away from the gang tracking us."

She had heard through the social grapevine that the Morgan brothers protected their own. She figured that was why this one was yet to be brought to justice. In her mind she classified them all as a gang, like the hole-in-the-wall gang. A group of men acting as a law unto themselves—renegades.

She knew the brothers would come, just as Mr. Morgan knew they would come. It was probably why he hadn't given her any trouble so far. That worried her more than she wanted to admit.

It meant that all her careful backtracking was probably for naught. Confound it! Doubling back had cost her precious time. Time she'd make up in the next few days even if she ran her own body to the ground.

The horses would be all right. Mr. Anderson, the blacksmith, assured her they were bred for hard riding and mountain terrain. The weakness in this whole game was herself.

She was a Boston girl born and bred. The orphanage was the only toughening she'd had. Sure she could shoot and use a knife, but she was stiff just from today's ride. In two or three days, she'd be so sore she wouldn't be able to raise her arms. How would she be able to shoot then? How could she maintain control over the tiger she currently held by the tail?

Brianna shook her head at her own negative thoughts. She was smart and she was fit. But mostly she was determined. A determined woman could do anything—even bring a huge and darkly handsome man across miles of wilderness. She would do it, too, but she'd worry until she had the reward money in hand.

*   *   *

She was gone long enough for Trey to get a grip on his overactive body. He'd slid down so the saddle was his headrest and stared up at the clear sky above him filled with stars. He realized that for the first time in years he felt alive.

So alive, he'd darn near kissed her.

He closed his eyes and wondered how she would have reacted if he had. Would she have kissed him back? Would she have held him close? Would she let him go?

He supposed he could get out of the ropes if he wanted to bad enough. But he didn't want to bad enough. No, he found it strangely seductive to be at her mercy. Or maybe it was simply that his insides were more tied up than his hands.

He wanted her.

But she was afraid of him; afraid of the killer she imagined she carried to justice. He wanted her to fear the killer she thought she had. It meant that she wasn't stupid.

One of the things he truly couldn't abide was a stupid woman. It was Katherine's cleverness more than her golden-haired beauty that had drawn him. It was that very same cleverness that masked a cold heart.

The bounty hunter was different. Katherine would have flirted, coaxed, and teased her way to her goal. Not the woman he had begun to think of as "Teach." No, she reached out and grabbed her goal and hung on tight. Trey lifted the corners of his mouth in a wry smile.

"Blast it!" he whispered. It took a strong a man to

handle that kind of woman. Good thing he was that kind of man.

His captor walked back into the small circle that was their makeshift camp. He watched her from the slit of his half-closed eyes. She didn't say a word, just sat down across from him and removed her boots. She lay down with her head on her saddle, wrapped a blanket around her, put her gun in her lap, and closed her eyes.

She just closed her eyes, dismissing him. Denying the fact that before she walked away from him, she'd been looking at him like most women eyed a piece of fancy chocolate. Like she wanted to eat him up. He couldn't help but wonder if she would go slow or gobble him all at once.

He shifted and realized he felt edgy and ornery. He didn't want her to ignore him. He wanted her to acknowledge him. "So, schoolteacher, what's your name?"

"Why?"

He shrugged. "Proper introductions. You get me clear to Durango, I'm going to want to know your name."

"Then I'll tell you when we get to Durango," she replied. "Go to sleep, Mr. Morgan." She closed her eyes.

He scowled at her. Women were talkers. They couldn't wait to express their every thought no matter how inane. That meant she was purposefully ignoring him.

He glanced up at the sky. If he figured right, his

brothers camped maybe five or ten miles away at the most. At this pace they'd find him by midday. Which meant he didn't have much time.

"Where are you from?" he pressed.

Silence filled the air between them. It was dark and icy. Some night animal rustled in the low brush. An owl screeched nearby, and still she didn't answer him. He knew she wasn't sleeping. Her breathing hadn't fallen into a regular pattern.

"So, wouldn't you want to know more about me?" he asked.

"I know everything I need to know about you," she said. Dismissal was very clear in her tone as her voice cut through the darkness.

If he weren't tied he could reach out and touch her. Bring her up against him and hold her. Kiss the top of her head and coax her into answering his questions.

"A wanted poster doesn't tell the whole story."

"I know more than the wanted poster."

"Prove it."

This time she turned her head and looked at him. "Why?"

He allowed a grin to slip over his features. "You can't, can you?" Satisfied with his conclusion, he closed his eyes. "Probably can't even shoot."

She blew out a long breath. "You're Robert Angus Morgan the third, born in 1863 to Robert Angus Morgan, Junior, and Patricia Harris Morgan."

"The wanted poster gave you my full name."

"You lived in Cheyenne with your Aunt Polly and went to school."

"There wasn't a school in Amesville," he countered, feeling a bit nettled that she would challenge his conclusion.

"Your mother wanted you to attend high school but your father called you home to learn the ranching business."

"Anyone could guess that. I own a ranch."

"While back in Amesville, you courted a number of girls off and on for a while, then in 1887, you decided to marry. Miss Katherine Dorn was the prize of the time. Slender, blue-eyed and blond-haired, she was the catch of the county. But something happened and she married another. You left home the next day with a pair of six-shooters, the Bowie knife, and a serious attitude."

"Rumors." He didn't like how confident she was.

"Your favorite color is green. Your favorite dinner is beef roast with new potatoes, and you'd fight anyone nearby for your Aunt May's apple pie."

"Enough," he ordered, as he sat up to glare at her. "Who the heck are you?"

"Good night, Mr. Morgan."

"I want to know who you are and why you know so darned much about me."

The sound of a six-shooter being cocked filled his ears. "Lay down," she ordered. "I can and will shoot this thing."

He threw himself back down and clenched his jaw in frustration. How did she know all that about him? How'd she know about Aunt May's pie? Who the heck was she?

Once again silence fell between them. He grumbled to the air in general about her being heartless, bossy, and unforgiving.

She laughed then. It was a clear bell tone of laughter that tickled his soul and filled his lonely heart.

"What's so funny?"

"You," she said simply and chuckled a bit longer before settling into silence. "Here you are, a wanted criminal trussed up like a thanksgiving turkey, muttering to the air because I won't talk to you."

"And how is that funny?"

"I thought men like you were the silent deadly type."

"Who says I'm not?"

She laughed again.

Irritated, he realized she'd tied him verbally as well as physically. If he said any more he'd prove her right. He'd be darned if he proved her right, because she was mistaken.

She fell silent yet again. This time it was longer, and darker. He gave up and at least pretended to sleep. If his instincts were correct, and they usually were, she was doing the same.

Thank God no one else was around to see him so thoroughly humiliated at the hands of such a charming reckless chit.

After nearly forty minutes of silence she spoke. He wasn't sure he heard her right and simply turned her way. She lay back with her hat tossed over her eyes, her head resting against her saddle. "It was the public library," she said. "I read about you in the library."

Well, shoot, he thought. That's right. His aunt was a member of Cheyenne society and loved to put everything in the paper. He had no idea the obscure little tidbits from the society pages would come back to haunt him.

She had him up before dawn the next day. She drove them harder than most men. She stopped only long enough to eat and rub down the horses. Meals consisted of beef jerky, water, and hard biscuits. By the third day he was hungry and tired and his hands and arms ached from being tied in strange positions.

His previous admiration for his brothers turned to disgust. The good-for-nothings were at least two days behind now. It was guaranteed they weren't riding as hard or as fast as she. Knowing Matt, he stopped every evening for fresh meat and a long, leisurely cigar.

At this rate they'd find Trey just about the time a hangman's noose fell around his neck. Idiots.

Trey didn't know how she did it but his schoolteacher seemed to know the mountains like the back of her own hand. She stopped and pulled out a small compass from time to time, studied the position of the sun, and dragged him up and over pass after pass.

He knew they were deep into Colorado. Heck, the way they were riding they'd be in Nevada in less than a week. He'd begun to feel the effects. His stomach growled and he was grumpier than a rattler disturbed from its midday nap.

What was worse was, he wasn't any closer to solving the puzzle she presented. Unlike every other female he'd ever met, this one didn't talk. She just ordered him to eat, sleep, and ride.

"You know how to talk without giving an order?" he asked when they stopped at the top of a ridge. Tall majestic mountains surrounded them, tops white with late snow, their sides purple in the shade or green in the sun.

She pulled out her compass. "There's water over the next ridge," she said. "We'll camp there for the night." She glanced at him.

"What kind of water?"

"A fair-sized stream according to the maps."

"What maps?"

"The maps in my head," she replied.

That startled him for a moment, but she never gave him time to retort. She simply pressed on. "We need to get moving or we'll arrive after dark."

He gritted his teeth at the jarring his lack of hands caused on his backside. "What are you going to do when we get there? Drown me?

"Of course not. Shooting is much more efficient."

"I've said it before and I'm going to say it again. You're a hard woman, Teach."

Over the next ridge, precisely where she said it would be was a spring-fed stream. She pulled up next to it and dismounted. "We'll camp here tonight," she announced. "The horses need to rest."

"Fine." He slid down off his horse without assistance. He'd become adept at it over the past few days and now she didn't even notice. It ticked him off.

Where was the woman who looked at him with admiration in her eyes?

He glanced her way as she pulled the heavy saddle off the horse and led it to the stream. She looked tired. It was the first time he'd really noticed.

Heck, if he were achy and tired, just how hard was this race on her? "We need fresh meat," he said. "We won't make it all the way to Durango on jerky and hard tack."

She didn't even look his way as she grabbed handfuls of grass and rubbed her horse down. He grumbled to himself about how she didn't listen.

He watched her work. Her hands were small but capable. She simply did what had to be done—no complaints, no discussion.

It bothered him that he was of little help. The best he could do was stay out of her way. His hands were cuffed behind him. It was pretty dang tough getting a saddle off with his hands tied behind him. It didn't stop him from trying.

"What are you doing?" she asked as she turned her hobbled horse free to range.

Trey was in a squat on his third attempt at unbuckling the cinch. "Caring for my horse."

"Sure, and I'm Queen Victoria," she said, her tone dripping with sarcasm.

He straightened. "That certainly explains your habit of ordering everyone around."

"I do not order everyone around. Now, go sit down."

He couldn't help the "I-told-you-so" grin that shot across his face.

She stopped in her tracks and narrowed her eyes. "I am not in the mood for an 'I told you so.'" She put her hands on her hips. "The horse needs to be cared for and there is little you can do."

"Untie my hands and I'll help."

She blew out a deep breath. It rustled the hair that had straggled loose from her thick braid. "That isn't likely to happen any time soon."

"Why not? Don't you trust me?" For some reason he really wanted her to trust him. In spite of the wanted poster. In spite of everything.

"Step away from the horse, Mr. Morgan."

"No."

"Fine," she said with a nonchalance he didn't like one bit and pulled out the gun. "Where shall I shoot you? Foot? Shoulder?" She bit on her lush bottom lip and eyed him critically. "Probably both to keep you down, but then I might as well kill you since we are rather far from a doctor." Her gorgeous green eyes looked through him clear to his soul. She raised the gun, pointed it at his heart, and pulled back the hammer. "I'll make it quick."

"Darn." He moved away. "You're crazy."

"Over by that tree, please."

He did what he was told. His feet had toughened a bit over the last few days. He barely felt the twigs and rocks that littered the ground. It had, however, ruined his socks. He eyed the hole that left his big toe exposed. His new sister-in-law Samantha would have a fit.

"Thank you." Teach said the words in perfect old maid pitch as she tucked the gun within easy reach. "Molly thanks you too."

He leaned against the tree and watched her work with quick, efficient movements. Her breasts swayed gently as she worked. It made his mouth water. He needed to distract himself. "Who's Molly?"

"Your horse," she replied and tossed the saddle and blankets down.

"My horse's name is Molly?"

"Yes."

"What's your horse's name?"

"Sophie."

He mulled that over while she rubbed Molly down, then hobbled her and left her to range a bit.

"What made you pick two mares?"

She turned and contemplated him. "One tough man was enough on this trip. Mares are more settled. Better suited for a long hard journey."

Astonished, he let his gaze run over her. She was coated in a fine dust that made her eyes greener but hid the fine porcelain of her skin. "You think females are really better at this kind of journey?"

"Certainly. We have more stamina."

"You're kidding, right?"

"As you should have figured out by now, Mr. Morgan, I rarely kid. Now, let's make our way down to the stream." She held out her hand and he spied a chunk of what looked like soap. "Cleanliness is next to godliness." She stopped to eye him thoughtfully. "You aren't afraid of a bit of godliness, are you?"

He straightened. If he didn't know better, he'd believe she just insulted him. "Can I shave?"

"I am not letting you have any kind of weapon. That includes a razor."

He moved away from the tree. "Fine. Then you shave me."

"Me?"

It was the first time he'd heard her squeak. "Why not? Are you afraid?" He was daring her.

"You should be the one afraid, Mr. Morgan."

"Call me Trey, will you?"

"Trey?"

"Yeah, for the third. Trey."

"I see. I suppose that's a colorful western name."

He paused and frowned at her. "What do you mean, colorful western name? You've got to be from around here too. Aren't you?"

Her gorgeous mouth thinned to a fine line. "It really doesn't matter where I'm from, now, does it? After all, we will part ways in Durango, never to meet again."

"Sure," he muttered, moving toward the stream. "Too bad we had to meet the first time."

He heard her breath intake at his jab. It didn't bring him pleasure. It made him feel guilty. She was working hard—harder than anyone he'd ever met. He had begun to respect her for that.

Katherine had never worked hard at anything. Not even flirting.

"Look, Teach, why don't you save us both a lot of trouble and tell me why you're taking me to Durango."

"There's a thousand-dollar reward for bringing you in."

"Honey, if this is about money, just set me free. I've got money."

"This is about more than money," she said as she pushed him toward the stream. "This is about dignity. This is about doing what's right. And I highly doubt that you know anything about that."

"You're wrong there." He suddenly wanted to tell her the truth. To somehow make her believe that he was not the man she thought he was. Instead he closed his mouth and walked to the stream.

He reminded himself that he had already learned that lesson. Women believed what they wanted to believe, nothing more, nothing less. It justified their actions.

She had kidnapped him. It would be her loss when she discovered the truth.

There was no reward waiting in Durango.

Chapter Four

Bri was tired, hot, sticky, and sore. She could have filled a dictionary with the words to describe how she felt. Worried was one of them. They weren't far enough away from their pursuers, but she had to rest. The horses had to rest. And Morgan was right: They needed fresh meat.

The water called her. Sparkling and cool, it gurgled to her. To heck with it, she'd have a bath first, then worry about the rest. She glanced at the man she followed, not fooled by his compliance. The gun in her hand was always loaded and she lived with an abnormal awareness of his every move. Always on guard, she anticipated any change in his breathing, any sign that he might have ideas about changing the balance of power.

So far, there had been not one sign of rebellion. She knew it must be because he was confident the gang would catch them. Still, he seemed more restless to-day, slower. Perhaps his confidence was slipping just a little.

At the edge of the stream she stopped him. Working quickly and efficiently, she tethered him to a nearby tree. She knew it wouldn't be safe for him to be free enough to bathe, but she couldn't deny him the cool water that called her. She decided to at least give him the shave he requested. So she took his hat and made her way to the stream.

"What are you going to do with that?" he asked.

"Use it as a basin," she replied. "You did want a shave, didn't you?"

"Only if you promise not to slit my throat."

"No promises," she shot back. "Close your eyes."

"Why?"

"It's the gentlemanly thing to do."

"I'm no gentleman."

His words were simple. Spoken in a deep dark tone that had the hairs at the back of her neck standing on edge again. Her knees quivered with a strange but de-licious emotion.

She denied her own reaction with a vengeance. "Fine." Shrugging, she backtracked toward him. She couldn't ever let him see any emotion, no matter how odd. She knew instinctively that the least bit of com-promise and he'd pounce.

"What are you going to do? Shoot me?"

"Nope." She pulled the kerchief off from around her neck and maneuvered around him. "Blindfold will do just as well." She placed the folded cloth around his eyes and tied hard.

"Hey."

He was big and warm and close. She savored the earthy scent of pine and horse and man. She stared at the width of his shoulders. Longing caused her to linger a bit too long until she felt compelled to touch him. She reached out, her fingers a breath away.

"Now, darlin', that's just cruel."

She jumped back and scrambled to her feet. "What?"

"Blindfolding a man. Don't you know it's cruel?"

She swallowed hard and chastised herself for day-dreaming. "It'll only be until I finish," she stated. "I won't take long."

That said, she picked up his hat and scurried close to the edge of the stream. With quick efficient movements, she stripped down to her drawers and camisole and put her toes in the water.

It was cold as ice. She gasped.

"What?" He sounded concerned; his head turned in her direction.

"It's just cold," she replied. Not nice and cool like it promised in its gurgles, but bone-chilling cold. It would be better if she simply jumped in. With a quick inhale, she dove into the stream. The shock of it hit her overworked body and drove all the air from her lungs.

She came up straight and true, breaking the surface with a gasp. She may have even muttered a curse.

She thought she heard him chuckle. But she didn't

have time to react. Her brain was quickly numbing along with her extremities. She soaped up fast and dipped to rinse, then made her way to the edge.

Bri no longer felt hot and itchy and tired. But she doubted she'd take another plunge in water quite that cold again.

"Must be really cold," he called. "I can hear your teeth chattering from here."

"You'll get your chance soon enough," she said, but the words were slightly slurred because her mouth had grown numb.

"No, thanks," he replied and leaned against the tree. "I think a shave will be quite enough."

She wasn't about to argue. She was freezing. Bri grabbed a blanket and wrapped it around her. She rummaged through her saddlebag and found a second set of underclothing. With the blanket as her shield, she stripped off her icy wet clothes and pulled on the dry ones, which promptly stuck to her skin.

She tugged on her petticoats, shirt, and skirt, then left her jacket hanging on the bush along with the wet underthings and the blanket that had absorbed most of the water. She belted her holster on her hip and resigned herself to combing her hair out later. Once she had a fire going and feeling back in her hands.

She strode over and tugged the blindfold off his face. He blinked, then eyed her damp but fully clothed body. "Don't look so disappointed," she said. "You might not be a gentleman, but I am a lady."

He allowed a slow and sexy grin to cross his face. "I expected nothing less, Teach."

A warmth spread through her at that look. She frowned and backed away. "Stop calling me that. I told you before. I'm not a teacher."

"Tell me your name."

The words were a quiet male command that made her heart flip.

"No."

"Why not?"

His gaze washed over her, heating the goosebumps that ran up and down her skin.

She should know how to handle that. It was the same kind of expression that Jimmy Dugan had used when he asked her to step out with him. Of course, he'd been all of seventeen and she sixteen. She'd handled him with a fist square in his face, but she doubted that reaction would work in this instance.

"Well?"

She tightened her mouth in her best spinster frown. "I do not make a habit of giving intimate details to men wanted for murder."

"Fine. I'll guess."

She shrugged and moved away. "Do what you like. I have work to do." Like gathering wood to start a fire to warm her hands and her feet.

"Emily."

She grabbed her stiff leather gloves and stuffed her fingers in. It wouldn't do to get blisters when she had so much riding ahead of her.

"Carolyn."

She checked her pistol and stuffed it in the waistband of her split skirt. After she made a fire she'd see about meat. Squirrel or rabbit would be best since she didn't want to waste anything.

"Irene."

Her wet braid had dripped water through her layers of clothing and now her back was cold. She glanced at the sky. The sun had gone over the mountains. If she didn't get going soon, she'd not have any light to see, and fresh meat would be a moot point.

"I'll be right back," she said. "Don't go anywhere."

"Shoot, I guess that means I can't take you for a stroll, Rebecca."

Confident, she turned and cast him a look that said he would never get it.

"Hey, a man's got to try."

She shook her head and hurried into the nearby woods. Aspens grew abundantly up here, and it wasn't long before she had an armload of seasoned wood. They wouldn't need much more than that since she didn't want to draw too much attention to their camp.

She returned to find him leaning against the tree scowling. "What?"

"You leaving me for bear bait?"

She moved toward a bare spot in the grasses and tossed the wood down. "Of course not, don't be silly."

"Funny, I feel like bear bait tied up to this tree."

"I'll untie you as soon as I get this fire going."

"I suppose you're going to use it to heat up more jerky. Where's the real meat?"

She sighed at the guilt that stabbed her and laid the fire. Soon it crackled with warmth. "It's gotten too dark to hunt, so you have your choice," she informed him. "Be free from that tree and eat cold jerky, or give me some time to make biscuits before I free you. I can't cook and hold a gun on you at the same time and I doubt you're ready to be hog tied for the night."

"What about my shave?"

"You're quickly becoming more trouble than you're worth."

"Then set me free, Susannah, and I'll hunt us up some meat and shave myself."

"Right, and I'll make myself a silk gown and meet you for dancing afterwards." She stood. "I don't think so."

"I've never known a lady with a mouth like yours."

"You aren't going to know this one either."

She walked over to her saddlebags and took out a pan, some flour, soda, salt, and fat back. At least they'd have biscuits. She was hungry, too, and knew she needed more food if she were going to make another day of hard riding.

"How about Elizabeth?"

She shook her head and moved back to the warmth of the fire.

"Constance."

She replied with silence.

"Abigail."

She did not acknowledge him.

"Give me a hint."

"No."

He quit then and she worked in silence. Kneading the biscuit dough helped her work the kinks out of her arms. She pinched and rolled the individual biscuits. Then she slipped the pan on the fire and sat back.

Her hair needed attention. It was still damp and she swore she could feel it tangling. So she went back to her saddlebags in search of her comb.

"Unhitch me, Amy," he said, his voice pleading with her, deepening her guilt. "I just want to be able to stand and stretch my legs."

She sighed and eyed her comb. If she unhitched him, she wouldn't be able to comb her hair. She couldn't trust any distractions. Hard heart, she had to have a hard heart if she was going to make it all the way to Nevada.

"Not yet," she said as firmly as possible. She grabbed a wide tooth comb and made her way back to the warmth of the fire. Her fingers were still slow due to the cold, but some time working her braid would help.

He grumbled something under his breath and sprawled back against the tree. She felt bad, but after all, he was a hardened criminal. When he got to Durango things would be even less comfortable for him in the jail.

She untied the bit of ribbon from the end of her waist-long braid and separated the hair. It was long and tedious work that she had become accustomed to. Her hair was thick but fine and tended to tangle when unattended.

They sat in silence. Her fingers worked her hair out of the braid as the fire snapped and popped and the biscuits cooked.

"I'm sorry about the lack of meat," she said, giving into her concern for his welfare. "I didn't see anything when I was gathering wood and it got too dark after that."

"Maybe you're not as good of a shot as you claim to be."

She brushed off his comment, though it hurt. They were both tired and sore. She had all the freedom, all the control. It had to grind on a man as commanding as Robert Morgan. So, he fought back with the only weapon he had: Words.

She worked her hair completely out and then began the slow process of combing it.

"Your hair looks red in the firelight, Amanda."

"It's an illusion," she replied. "It's brown." She pulled the comb through the lower third. "Serviceable brown, average. Well, maybe a little unruly."

"Sort of like you then," he replied.

Sadness stabbed her and she stopped and turned to look at him. "No one's ever called me serviceable before."

"I meant unruly."

She turned back to the flame and continued to work the tangles. "I see. Well, I suppose that would be your point of view."

"Stubborn, too," he replied. "If you had a temper I'd swear you were a true redhead."

She had to laugh at that. "One thing I don't have much of is a temper." She unknotted the final tangles and ran the comb through her hair. "I don't get angry, Mr. Morgan." She turned and eyed him. "I get even."

That said, she reached over and turned the biscuit pan so that it would brown evenly. Then she quickly rebraided her hair and tied the ribbon soundly on the end.

"I've never known a woman like you."

She couldn't tell if that was a good thing or a bad thing. She stood, brushing off her clothes. "I suppose that's about the most honest thing you've ever said to me." She drew a deep breath. "For that you get a reward."

"Are you going to untie me?"

"No, I'm going to do what you suggested and give you a shave." She grabbed his hat, filled it with water, her chunk of soap, and the razor out of her pack. "Shall we see if I'm as good with a blade as I say I am?"

He sat up cross-legged, his hands still tied behind him, and watched while she approached. "Do you know what you're doing?"

She set the instruments down and looked him square in the eye. "I haven't a clue as to what I'm doing. So, if you want to save your face, you'd better talk me through this."

He eyed her suspiciously. "You'd trust me to do that?"

"Of course. It's your throat."

"True."

The night around them was quiet except for the crackle and occasional pop of the flames. She was aware of the smell of seasoned wood, baking biscuits, and man. "So? What do I do first?"

"First you'll have to get closer than that."

She frowned and moved the hat and towel closer, but still kept the razor at a distance.

"I can't grab it," he said quietly. "My hands are tied behind my back."

She realized he was right. There was such a thing as too much caution. Still, she didn't like being so close to him. It made her feel odd. She kind of liked it. That was bad, very bad. It meant he had begun to charm her.

Her brother needed the money more than she needed to be charmed. She had to keep that thought in her head. It seemed to slip away the closer she got to the man.

She looked to him for guidance. He watched her. His bright blue gaze seduced her heart, making her want to lean closer.

"First off you have to wet my beard."

She dipped a corner of the towel in the cold water and dabbed at his face. His skin was as she imagined—warm, his beard rough.

"Wetter."

She frowned again and soaked up more water, sousing him. He grinned. "That's my girl."

She leaned away from him. "Don't call me that."

"What?" He made the comment sound innocent but they both knew what she meant.

"I am not now, nor will I ever be your girl. Now, I believe I need to lather next," she said and twisted the soap between her palms until she worked up a tiny bit of lather. Then she looked from her hands to his dripping jaw and realized she'd have to touch him.

She bit her bottom lip and held her breath. Touching him would make him even more real. So far she'd managed to keep a polite distance. He was tied up. He was a criminal. She had concentrated on not thinking past the thousand dollars she would need for her brother's freedom. It had helped her keep her distance.

"Maybe this isn't a good thing," she said and leaned over to rinse her hands in his hat.

"Wait!" He stopped her with the urgency of his voice. "You promised me at least a shave."

She looked at him. He had to be as hot and sticky as she had been before her short bath. She couldn't do it. She couldn't deny him this little bit of comfort just because she was afraid.

"There isn't much lather in this soap."

He shrugged. "It's better than nothing."

"Will you think that when I slice you to ribbons?"

"I trust you'll be gentle."

"It might be less painful if I shoot you first."

"That's a chance I'm willing to take."

"Fine."

"Fine."

She tried to lather the soap again. This time she got a bit more. Quickly she turned and rubbed the lather into his beard. His face was warm and bristly. The hairs had softened in the water.

She grabbed the soap again and worked it, then applied it. His skin was sensual to her touch. Her palms savored the texture and contours of his face. She breathed in his rich scent as she leaned closer trying to catch all the places along his jaw.

"There," she said and leaned back to inspect her handiwork. They were mere inches apart now. She practically sat in his lap; yet she was drawn closer. He drew her like magnet to metal.

"You bite your lip when you concentrate," he said, his tone low and husky.

"I beg your pardon?"

His gaze flew up from her mouth to her eyes. "Did you know you bite your bottom lip when you concentrate?"

The question turned her guts to jelly. "I had no idea," she answered low and soft.

She wove toward him like a snake to a snake charmer. They were the only two people on the earth tucked away safe on the side of a mountain and she wanted, no, needed to touch him. Her palms ached to explore further the contours of his face, his neck, and his shoulders.

He must have sensed her need. "Untie me." She blinked. It had been a soft command. The demand of a lover. Her heart pounded, her hands ached and she wanted to slide right down on top of him. But he was tied. Why was he tied?

Reality returned with a rush.

"No." She pulled away and took a deep breath, trying to clear her mind. "No."

"Why?"

She swallowed. The question had been another

coax, more charm, and his expression tugged at her heart.

"I can't." She imagined Eve in paradise being se-duced by the snake. The fruit looked good enough to bite. She was Eve. If she bit this apple, there would be heck to pay. She had to be strong.

Bri reached for the razor and held the cold, cool metal in her hand, twisting it until it fit between her fingers. "You're losing lather," she commented as she eyed his face.

"You're kiliing me," he grumbled under his breath.

"Not yet," she replied grimly and looked him square in the eye. "I believe I'm supposed to scrape this razor over your throat."

He swallowed visibly. "Darlin', whenever you're ready."

She eyed him suspiciously. "Won't I cut you?"

"You can't wound me any more than you already have."

She frowned. "Are your ropes too tight?"

"No, they're just fine."

She narrowed her eyes. "I will never set you free."

He watched her, his gaze reaching into the depths of her soul. "You don't see me complaining, do you?"

"Hmmmm, why is that?"

"I smell something burning," he said, changing the subject.

"What?"

He nodded toward the fire. "I believe the biscuits are burning."

"Shoot." She hopped up, grabbed the corner of her

split skirt, and nudged the biscuits off the fire. The smell of charred bread filled her nostrils and she sighed.

"Well, you might be handy with a gun, but you don't know much about cooking."

Disgusted, she straightened from the ruined biscuits and wielded the razor. "You distracted me."

"Maybe."

"Just for that I'm shaving you, lather or no."

He acquiesced with a dip of his head. "Probably for the best."

She shook her head at the ruined meal and felt her stomach rumble at the loss. She should have known he would distract her. Well, live and learn.

She knelt down. With a firm hand she grabbed his ornery chin and took a long swipe of the razor up the side of his neck. It cleared the hairs in one easy motion. She wiped the side of the razor on his thigh. He flinched and she studied him.

"What?"

"A might close."

She eyed the shave line critically. "No, it looks good to me." She ran her hand along the spot and felt smooth warm skin. "No nicks."

"I didn't mean my face," he replied matter-of-factly.

She frowned a moment, then blinked. "Oh." She had wiped the razor down close to his lap. Embarrassed, she felt the heat of a blush rush up her face. "I'll be more careful."

He answered with a muffled, "Hmmm."

She had already grabbed his chin and made another

swipe. It was best to get this business over with. So she could go back to the other side of the campfire. Then they could dine on burnt biscuits and jerky and pretend to sleep.

Night swallowed them completely while she concentrated on the shave. Toward the end, it was hard to tell what was what, and she worked on feel as much as sight. He never flinched or complained and she was careful not to leave any scars.

"Done," she said with relief.

"Thank you," he said simply.

"You're welcome." She rocked back on her heels and cleaned the razor before she put it away. "Let's have those biscuits."

"Teach," he said, stopping her with his tone of voice.

"What?"

"Thanks, really. I'm sorry about the biscuit comment."

"It happens even in the best kitchens, if the pot isn't watched."

Suddenly there was a noise from the edge of the camp. Bri stood, her gun in her hand. She held her other hand out to caution him to keep quiet.

He made no sound. It was as if the whole world held its breath. Then a slight movement caught her eye. She saw the flash of red. Critter eyes. Drawing up the gun she shot where she estimated the heart to be.

The sound reverberated around them. The smell of gunpowder drifted up from the gun as she lowered it to her side. She held her finger to her lips and Trey nodded.

Then she slowly made her way to the edge of camp. Nothing else moved. Even the crickets stopped singing at the sound of the gun. Bri's heart pounded in her head. She eased toward where she had shot. The flickering firelight bounced off the body of a rabbit.

She relaxed almost instantly. "Looks like there'll be meat after all," she said. She reached down and grabbed the rabbit by its ears and turned to show him.

"Nice shot."

Bri put her gun back into her holster and pulled out her knife. "This will make up for the burnt biscuits."

"I suppose this means I won't be unhitched for a while."

She tilted the corner of her mouth in thought. "I'm afraid it does. I need both hands to clean and spit the meat. I don't want to risk charring it as well."

He shrugged and leaned back against the tree. "Kind of getting used to being cramped."

"We could eat jerky," she pointed out.

"I'll wait."

Chapter Five

She was the meanest woman he'd ever known. That was what he liked best about her.

His captor always spoke the truth, never once lying for comfort, flirting for money, or pretending she needed him when she didn't.

Truth was, she needed him. If for nothing else, to get the thousand dollars she saw as the price on his head. He kicked around telling her it wasn't going to happen, but he decided she wouldn't believe him. Not yet. Then if she did believe him, he was half afraid she'd shoot him anyway.

He grinned at that thought, then sobered. Her reacting times were almost as good as his brother Tag's. He hadn't even seen the gun get into her hand. It was just there from one moment to the next, like breathing.

He wondered what she had faced in her life that she had had to learn to wear a gun. A woman like her should be holding children and soothing hurts. She had gentle hands, capable hands. Her touch had excited him more than he'd ever been in his life, and all she'd done was shave his face.

A smooth, clean, nick-free shave, done with care.

It would have scared the bejeebers out of her had she known what he was thinking while he watched her work. It half scared him. His thoughts hadn't been purely sensual. They'd been . . . possessive.

Trey finished his duty, buttoned his fly, and turned back to camp. She had unhitched him before too long and retied his hands forward so he could eat and stretch and take care of his own matters.

Still she watched him, and since he saw her peg that rabbit in the half-light of a fire, he had more respect for her skill with the gun.

He figured it was his charm that had kept him alive this far. He grinned. With any luck it would stand him in good stead and keep him alive until they reached Durango or his brothers rescued him.

He stopped in front of her and held out his hands. "Just like a pig preparing to be slaughtered," he commented dryly.

"It's not that bad," she replied. "Maybe a little un-comfortable—"

He snorted.

"But not torture."

She hopped off the rock that had served as her vantage point and approached him cautiously. He noticed that about her. She was not given to wild leaps of faith or hot-headed passions. No, everything about her was well thought out. Even her decision not to give him her name.

If he were a real criminal, he might be angry enough to track her. Given a name it would be fairly easy. Then the tables would be turned.

Smart. She was very smart. She kept her mouth shut. It must be killing her.

He felt the edge of a knife in his kidneys and low-ered his cuffed hands out in front of him. She kept the knife firm and steady as she unlocked the handcuffs.

"Raise them slow," she said, her tone even, and husky. He wanted to do a lot of things slow with his hands; raising them was not one of them.

She slid around him. The knife moved with her, never leaving contact with his body, yet never break-ing the skin.

"Okay, behind the back."

With great care and caution, he placed his hands behind his back. "You can put down the knife. I won't try to hurt you."

He felt a strong tug as she pulled his arms back and completed the ritual of hog-tying him before bed. He'd have to get the troubling thoughts out of his brain right away or he'd be uncomfortable for a very long time.

"Right. Now think about it. If I was a woman you loved—"

He swung his head around quick at her words. "What?"

His motion must have frightened her. She slid the knife so that the point drew blood. "Don't move."

He froze.

She took a steadying breath. "Do you plan on moving?"

"No."

"Good." She replaced the knife so that the long edge of the blade skimmed his skin above his kidneys and then went back to work on the ropes. "Let me start over. If your mother was out in the wilderness with a man she was not married to and she had the choice to keep him tied or not, what would you advise her to do?"

"Untie him, let him take care of her."

"What if he were an accused murderer, a man whose crimes were so heinous they had heaped a thousand-dollar reward on his head?"

She finished and stepped around him. Out of habit Trey tested the strength of the knots; as usual they held secure. His hands were tied behind him, then a second rope tied his hands to his waist and finally to the back of one ankle. If he tried to run he'd break his arms. But if he walked slow, he could lie down.

"Well?"

He scowled at her. The very idea that his mother would be alone with a murderer gave him chills. "If my mother had ever gotten close to such a man, I'd have told her to shoot him and ask questions later."

She watched him. Her beautiful eyes normally so expressive were carefully blank. "I don't really want to have to do that," she said and stepped away.

"I see," he said. "You still don't trust me."

There was a long uncomfortable silence he wasn't sure how to read.

"I made you a bedroll," she finally said in reply and pointed to a blanketed area. "We're up high enough that the ground gets cold at night. I think you're clever enough to figure out how to get between the blankets."

He blew out a breath. She wasn't ready to kill him yet, but neither did she trust him. He wondered if she ever would. And if she did, could he trust her in return?

The fire died slowly, surrendering to the cold mountain night. Bri cleaned her guns and sharpened the edge of her knife. She had learned one thing about weapons. They weren't any good if you didn't take care of them.

Right now with her belly full of meat and soft biscuit, she felt like she could sleep for a week. She stared up at the spectacle of stars that studded the sky like snowflakes, cold, twinkling and out of reach.

She wondered what her brother was doing. Those foul men had better be taking good care of him. She ran her thumb along the edge of her pistol. The lure of a thousand dollars should be more than enough to keep her brother safe. It was her only hope.

She put down the gun and looked over to find Trey Morgan watching her in the dim glow of the coals. His dark eyes sparked like the stars and a surge of heat and pleasure ran through her, thickening her pulse and making her feel utterly female.

It was the strangest thing. Something she hadn't even considered. She'd never experienced feelings like this before and, therefore, wasn't sure how to react.

Once you catch a tiger, what do you do if he seduces you?

"You must be cold." His words floated softly on the night.

She snuggled into her blankets. She had on three petticoats, her split skirt, camisole, shirt, and jacket under the blankets. It wasn't the most comfortable, but it kept the cold out. "You have fewer clothes," she observed. "I'm probably warmer."

"It would be better if we slept together and pooled our heat."

The idea actually appealed to her. That was bad. That was real bad.

"Lie down with the dogs, wake up flea-bitten."

"I take it that's a no," he said dryly.

"You would be correct."

She saw him turn his face away and watched his profile. The old beard growth had begun to blur the fine line of his jaw. She decided she liked him better clean-shaven.

The memory of the texture of his beard, the heat and softness of his skin on her fingers made her hands itch. She rubbed them together trying to banish it. It didn't work.

"It's not as if I could touch you tied like this," he remarked dryly. "Use your common sense. It's been known to snow up here even in July."

"I am using common sense," she replied. "If I got comfortable, I might sleep too long," she explained. "We have to be up and moving at dawn. We have a lot of ground to cover yet and your gang is still closer than I want them to be."

He glanced her way and raised an eyebrow. "My gang?"

"Your brothers. If they're keeping an even pace they're about a day's ride back." She took a deep breath and snuggled deeper, trying to ignore the cold seeping up her feet.

"What makes you think we haven't lost them?" he asked. "You've doubled back more than once and we're riding hard, darn hard."

"They're still coming." His lack of concern made her certain about her assumptions. If his brothers weren't close he wouldn't be so comfortable. He had a lot of confidence in how good they were. She had to be better than them.

"Tell me your name." He broke into her thoughts, speaking gently. "A nickname even—something." He paused and she felt her heartstrings tug at the sound of his request. He was so earnest.

"Bri," she said. Her voice was quiet and tiny in the giant stillness of the night. Her heart pounded at the risk she took. If he called her by her name, he would become more and more real. The more he became a person to her, the harder it would be for her to turn him in.

She was already coming to care for him more than she should. She wanted to be able to turn him in and take the money with no regrets. But she knew that she would regret it. After all, who knew what they would do to him? She swallowed hard. They may even hang him.

Tears welled up in her eyes. What a choice. Rescue her brother or send an intelligent gentle man to his death.

"Bri," he replied as secretively as she. Their voices could barely be heard in the thundering of her heart.

"Are you crying?"

The question brought up a well of emotion. Tears spilled over her cheeks and—darn it—she needed to sniff.

She rolled over on her side and wiped her nose as she turned. "Good night."

After a few moments of silence he answered, not in triumph but with meaning. "Good night, Bri."

She had them up before the sun had broken over the tops of the mountains. He saw the stiffness in her walk. The sure but slow way her hands saddled the horses. Anger surged through him. She was tired and sore and, by God, she was cold. The woman had the sense and stubbornness of a mule.

"This is madness," he declared. "You're killing yourself."

She packed up the camp gear and checked to make sure the fire was out. "I'm fine," she said while she worked. Then she shot him a glance. "If you think you can't make it, just let me know and I'll put you out of your misery."

He answered her with a black scowl, which she ignored. Instead she skillfully hid any traces of the camp. It wouldn't do her any good. Matt would find the camp.

She stopped and saw him scowling at her. "I suppose you think I'm wasting my time," she said.

"You are." He straightened as best he could. Maybe he could intimidate her a bit with his height.

It didn't work.

"Of course, your brothers will see through this," she said with a wave of her hand. "I'm not doing it for them."

That caught his attention. "No?"

"No." She moved matter-of-factly toward him. "Turn." Again the knife threatened his kidney. He allowed her to untie him from his night restraints.

"Then who?"

"According to the books, this area is well traveled by Indians."

He grinned at the ridiculous idea that Indians might track them. Then he just as quickly sobered. She was right in one respect. Outlaw bands would be hungry and angry and therefore very dangerous. "Just where in the heck are we?"

She cuffed him for riding. "We're in Utah, about two hundred miles from Durango. Beyond the miners and just outside the edge of civilization."

The sense of danger crept down his spine. They were not in a good place. "Why didn't you take the train out of Denver?" he growled.

"I did it for your safety as much as mine," she said and mounted her horse.

"My safety? What's safe about the middle of renegade Indian country?"

She pulled the ever-present pistol and pointed it at him. "Mount up."

He grumbled under his breath and did what she asked. "You are certifiable. I swear they should lock you up in an asylum somewhere." Settling himself on top of the horse, he continued. "What are you protecting me from anyway?"

She didn't even glance his way. Instead she started the horses into a zigzag pattern over the ground. He knew the trick. It made it look like there were many more than two horses here. Enough to make anyone who stumbled across the area think twice before they tried to ambush them.

"Well?" he nearly shouted, his temper rising with her damned silence.

"It's who, not what. I'm not the only one who has seen that wanted poster. Tied up like that you are an easy mark."

"I see," he said bitterly. "You didn't want anyone to get your reward."

She stopped and looked him dead on. "I didn't want to see you killed."

The sincerity in her voice gave him pause. That was twice she said she didn't want to kill him. He was beginning to believe she really meant it.

She kicked the horses into a hard gallop and started up and over the mountain. "Don't even think that I'm getting soft," she shouted over her shoulder. "I will shoot you faster than last night's rabbit if I have to."

* * *

They rode as hard as possible up the mountains, carefully down, then lightning fast across the broad valleys. Bri stopped only long enough to water the horses. Dinner was leftover biscuits and jerky.

She drove them like the Seventh Cavalry was after them, desperate as she was to cover as many miles as possible. Right now she hurt in so many places she wasn't sure she'd be able to get up in the morning. Every time her backside hit the saddle it pained her. Her arms and legs felt frozen into place, and still she pushed on.

Knights on quests worked through the toughest of tests. She had expected to hurt. She hadn't expected to ache this much. She'd have to rub her muscles with horse liniment tonight or she'd never make it through another day.

She half grinned. At least the smell of the liniment would discourage her handsome captive from trying to sleep with her. The grin faded. She had never been so tempted in her life. She glanced back. He rode straight and true. She had his horse's reins, but he didn't need them. His strong thighs clasped the beast, sending silent signals.

It would be so easy to love a man of such strength and cunning. She knew it deep in her heart. He could have survived the orphanage. In fact, he'd have been the leader after his second day. Instinctively she knew he would have protected the girls and the smaller boys.

She pressed on. Then why was his name and that scowling handsome face on a wanted poster? Maybe she'd ask him tonight. After all, there had to be a story attached to that wanted poster.

No, she firmly chastised herself. Any story would make him more human. She had a big heart. He would easily sucker her into letting him go. Then where would she be?

Her thoughts turned to her brother. Ethan looked so small and bruised when she had last seen him. She glanced at her captive. In contrast he was big and bold and full of health.

He could take care of himself. Ethan couldn't. The choice was simple. She must choose the boys. No regrets.

They rode until the sun set over the western mountains. The stands of pines were cool at this altitude. Today they had skirted several patches of snow, some filled with tracks of many creatures. others pristine and pure in the shining sun.

She called camp near a small stream. So far, the surveyors' maps had held true. Each creek was precisely where they had said. And they were making good time.

Now all she had to do was get off the horse and make camp without revealing just how sore she was.

He simply slid off his horse, his form as graceful as a cat's. She told herself to ignore him. She had work to do. He took up watch near a set of boulders.

"You're pushing yourself too hard," he noted. "You need to slow down or we'll both be dead before we get to Durango."

Tired, she brushed the hair out of her eyes and

worked on the horses. Twilight danced around them, bringing with it the cold fresh air and a scent of rain.

"It's best to keep moving."

Suddenly he was behind her. She felt the heat emanating from his body and froze. He inched closer. Her heart pounded in fear and something else. All the hairs on the back of her neck rose to signal danger; but it wasn't the danger of a criminal. No, it was the danger of a man surrounding a woman.

Heat pooled in her stomach and raced through her body. She wrapped her hand around the handle of her knife, but did not draw it. Time was suspended as she waited—spellbound by his nearness, enticed by his scent.

"Easy," he whispered. "Easy. I promise I won't ever hurt you." She inhaled sharply as he planted a soft kiss on the bare skin just under her ear. That small space between her hair and her collar was exposed, and he took it. His firm lips were warm, sending heat lightning clear to her toes.

She gripped the knife handle, knowing she should stop him, wanting him to go on kissing her. Yet encouraging him would only be madness on her part.

"You taste sweet like candy, warm like woman," he said next to her ear. Another round of goosebumps danced along her skin and along with it was a longing so deep, so strong, it made her weak. She wavered in the temptation, wanting to lean against his broad chest, to find out more about this pleasure his lips had teased from her.

"Please." The word torn from her was both invitation and exhortation.

He planted one more sweet caress on her skin. She felt her knees buckle and the horse shift.

Sanity returned in an instant. She whipped the knife from its sheath; but her reactions were dulled by pleasure.

He already stood a yard away, his eyes narrowed and hidden under the shadow of his hat. She brandished the knife between them. The threat was not what it should be. Her hands shook visibly.

She took a deep breath, sucking in the cool mountain air. It was a sad attempt to clear her muddled brain. He simply watched her as if he'd never seen her before.

She felt the loss of his heat and the pleasure of him as finely as her own pulse. Her body warred with her mind, wanting to go to him. She eyed him warily.

He didn't move. The lightning between them continued. She had to break the spell, had to take command of this situation—or her whole quest would fail.

She took another draught of air and narrowed her eyes. "Why did you do that?"

He shrugged. The movement was slow and insolent. "I've been wanting to do that for a long time."

She straightened, anger replacing confusion. "This is not about what you want," she snapped.

"No," he replied, his tone exposing his own anger. "This is about what you want."

His anger hit her hard. She shook it off and put the

knife away. "No, it is bigger than both of us." She withdrew her six-shooter. "Move over to that tree."

He eyed her weapon. She drew back the hammer with an audible click. He turned and moved to where she placed him. She worked quickly to tether him to the tree. Her wanton body warmed the second she got within two feet of him, her gaze caught by the breadth of his shoulders, the way his clothes draped over his backside. It just made her angrier.

Without looking back, she strode to the horses, put the gun away, and went back to work.

It was dark by the time she finished and tossed the bedrolls down on the ground. "No fire tonight," she said as she untied him from the tree. "So make it quick." He allowed her to change the handcuffs from the back to front before he sauntered off into the bush. "Far enough." She kept her tone stiff and distant. She had to work at it to mentally distance herself from him. Every muscle in her body pleaded with her to slow down and rest. What had happened tonight showed her she couldn't take that chance. The man was more dangerous to her than she had ever dreamed.

Trey was so in tune with her that he sensed her restlessness and worry from ten feet away. He frowned. He shouldn't have done what he did. It scared her.

His mind went back to the moment when he'd followed his gut reaction and stepped in behind her. Even with her as his captor, he wanted her.

It had become a game he played in his mind. He

had been thinking about how he could kiss her. He'd imagined many scenarios. But none had been as purely sensual as the reality, when he'd managed to actually touch her.

Her skin was soft as velvet and headier than fine wine. He licked his lips, the kiss still fresh in his mind. He'd kissed other women, but none had been that sweet, that fresh.

Katherine had been perfectly perfumed and powdered. He'd rarely gotten a taste of the true woman under all her manners. At the time he'd been too obsessed to see that. But years of experience had taught him that people hid under their manners. It was something Bri—his Bri—didn't do.

He released a deep breath when his body tightened again at the direction of his thoughts. Something had definitely changed today, something deep inside him. He knew she felt it. He could tell by the distance she now kept between them. She wanted him too.

He savored the notion. All she had to do was ask him if he were innocent and he'd explain the whole thing. Then she could take off these darn cuffs and ropes and he'd show her just how right they were for each other.

Chapter Six

He should never have kissed her. It stood between them like a wounded elephant. She stayed on the opposite end of the camp and refused to talk to him, as if she were afraid of him. Or maybe she was afraid of herself. Even though he liked that idea, he knew that if this kept up, she just might get nervous enough to start shooting.

"Why do you need the money?" he asked.

The question ricocheted through the crisp night air. She instantly ceased her restless movement.

"I beg your pardon?"

Trey winced at her tone. It was cool and unfeeling. And he was too far away to heat it up. He shifted. Maybe it was better that way. "I was wondering what would make a woman come nine hundred miles to face down a criminal and drag him back. I figure it ain't just for justice."

She stiffened as if he had insulted her. Good—it would give her something new to think about. Something to distract her from worrying about that kiss.

"How do you know it's not for justice?" She sounded indignant.

He grinned into the darkness. "I just know." He paused to let that sink in. "So, if it ain't for justice, then it's for money." The memory of another woman using him for money shot through him like hot lead. He willed the thought away. Katherine had not been honest about it. Bri was nothing if not straightforward.

He listened to the stillness, aware of her brain working as she tried to find an answer she could live with. He cut off her thoughts. "Here's the way I figure it. You need a huge sum of money and so you came up with this harebrained idea."

That got her goat. She sat straight up. "First of all, I am not harebrained and you are blind if you haven't noticed. Second, I have a very good reason for needing the money, and it's not for new dresses."

He softened at her anger. "I didn't figure it was for a dress, darlin'." He drawled soft as a man croons to a half–wild colt. "So, tell me what you need the money for."

She let out a long sigh. "Why?" she asked. Her loneliness and frustration were evident in her tone. "Why do you care?"

"It's my life on the line," he said. "I figure I have the right to know why I'm being sacrificed."

She tucked her knees up and rested her chin on them. The thin blanket shielded her from his gaze. He waited. She would answer this question. He knew she would. She was made of honorable stuff.

"You aren't being sacrificed," she said, her gaze puzzling over the space in front of her. "You're a wanted man." She turned to him and he could see the sparkle of her eyes in the starlight. "What happened? What made you go from the respected son of a prominent family to a wanted criminal?"

Shoot, she could turn a subject quick. Firmly hogtied, he was never more exposed than he was right now.

"I know that's a personal question," she said and turned back to stare out into the darkness. "You don't have to answer. As for me, all I can tell you is that you're right. I'm doing this for the money, but I'm not sacrificing you. I'm bringing you to justice, which is a lot more than most bounty hunters would have done." She turned her gaze back onto him. "Most would have shot you first and asked questions later."

"No one else has ever gotten this close to me," he said. Then he paused and thought through what he wanted to say. "I was betrayed by my fiancée. She left me for a richer man."

"That's pretty cliché, isn't it?" she asked.

Her reaction stopped him short. Okay, she was an educated woman. He knew that much about her, the library, the use of the word cliché. Where was she from? He couldn't even place her accent. She'd done a good job of hiding it. But not good enough.

"She was pregnant with my child at the time," he said quietly. The words didn't hurt any more. The meaning, which had grown cold and empty over time, still left a bitter taste in his mouth.

"I'm sorry. . . . Surely she didn't convince the other man the child was his."

"She didn't. She 'miscarried.' " His chest still tightened with anger and regret at this thought. The thought that money would make a woman lose her child, *his* child.

Silence wove between them, fresh as the night air.

"I'm sorry. Perhaps it was for the best."

"The only one it was best for was Katherine. She didn't tell me about the child. One day she went to see the midwife and within a day she lost the baby. She married her wealthy idiot two weeks later. I heard they moved out to San Francisco."

"You think it was on purpose, so you turned to a life of crime."

"Look, I'm going to be honest with you. I'm not a criminal."

"Yes, you are. I have the wanted poster."

He shook his head at the stubborn turn in her voice. "No, I'm not. I went to ground for a few years. Fed my anger with whiskey and fast women; kept people away with the threat of the Bowie and the six-shooters. But I never committed a crime."

"Then why the wanted poster?" she demanded. "No one gets a thousand-dollar reward on their head for no reason."

"I built up a reputation, because I was mean. I didn't let anyone get close. The reputation was useful. Kept most idiots away."

"And the thousand dollars?"

"My brothers thought it was time I came home. My ma had died and Matt'd been looking after my ranch. It'd been five years. It was time."

"So, why didn't they just come get you?" Her voice rose with every word.

"Calm down, sweetheart."

She whirled. "No I won't calm down and don't call me that!"

"Fine, darlin'."

She glared at him. He wondered if she knew the effect was lost in the dark of the night. "What has that got to do with the reward?"

"Matt posted it. He figured it would bring me home."

"Well, that's just plain stupid. It could have gotten you killed. Do you know how many uneducated idiots are out here passing themselves off as bounty hunters? I bet most of them can't even read. But I know that thousand dollars sticks out enough to bring half the country after you."

He was charmed by her concern for him, but a bit offended that she didn't believe he could handle himself. "I was never in any danger."

"Right," she waved her hand dramatically. "That's why you're tied up like a hog right now."

"Darlin', you can tie me up any time you want."

She shoved her hand through her hair. "So you're telling me there is no reward."

"Matt paid the sheriff when I was brought in," Trey

said. "A notice went out telling everyone the bounty was paid."

"If that were true, why would you let me get this far?"

"At first I didn't think it would go this far." He shrugged. "Then I was curious. Wondered if you could do it. Wondered why you'd do it."

She plopped back on her bedroll. "I don't believe you. I can't believe you." Her words became a whisper. "I can't. It's too important."

"Tell me what you need the money for. I can help."

She looked at him. He could almost hear her thinking. That was not a good sign. "You are a charming man when you want to be," she stated.

"Thank you."

"So was the snake in the bible."

He knew he was in trouble. "Aw, come on, darlin', why would I lie to you?"

"Why indeed," she replied softly. She slipped her hands behind her head. It was a thoughtful pose, a sexy pose to his way of thinking. He could make out the thrust of her soft breasts, the jut of her chin, the soft profile of her lips. Drats! He wanted her to see him as her savior, not her salvation. He was a man, after all, not a stray animal being returned for a reward.

He needed to be with her, close to her, as close as man and woman could possibly get. Give her something else to think about. But he couldn't do that until she trusted him.

On the one hand he was desperate for her to trust

him, let him get close, maybe even let him help her with her problem. On the other, he didn't want her to be so stupid as to be sweet-talked by some criminal even if the supposed criminal was him.

"Heck of a situation," he muttered.

"What?"

"Look, just rest here for a few days, my brothers will show up and verify the story."

She sighed and the sound carried to him. "Right. Stay here and let your gang overpower me. I don't think so. Good night, Mr. Morgan."

He scowled. It was a no-win situation. He was doomed if he did and doomed if he didn't.

"What will you do when you get to Durango and find out the money was already paid?"

She rolled away from him and dragged the blanket up over her shoulder. "I guess that's a chance I'll have to take. But I don't believe you, not for a minute. Goodnight." She sounded small and vulnerable and, for the first time, unsure of herself.

He eyed her from the back, how her waist curved in and her hip flared gently. He wanted so bad to feel that curve with his hands, curl himself around her and make all her problems go away.

He was as much a fool as she was.

The next two days were a grueling testament to her memory. The mountain passes proved rockier than described. At one point they had to get off the horses and lead them through a narrow crevice from one canyon to the next. They had gotten far enough down the mountainside that it was hot, and she was cranky.

Still her memory served her well. There was supposed to be a creek over the next ridge. She imagined the cold clear mountain water and dreamed about how good it would feel against her skin.

Anything to forget the conversation they'd had in the dark that night and the memory of his lips along her neck. The thought brought goosebumps to her even now.

If he was an innocent man—heck, who was she kidding, she wanted him to be an innocent man. Right now, if she didn't have to worry about her brother, she'd untie the man and throw herself into those big strong arms. Just to see what other kinds of pleasures he'd think up for her.

Blast, it was getting hot. She paused at the edge of the ridge and looked back. He never wavered, never berated her. Simply followed as silent and strong as an Indian.

It made her feel protected, not afraid. Oh, no, she was becoming far too attached to the tiger. "Stupid," she whispered.

He looked up. "What?"

She blinked and covered her tracks. "There should be a stream up about four hundred yards." She kept her tone brisk, anything to keep him from seeing what she was really thinking. "We should be able to stop and give the horses a good drink."

His dark eyes squinted against the sun. His lower

face was once again filled with the rough growth of beard.

She couldn't help remembering what it was like to shave that beard, to feel the heat and smell the scent of his skin. She swallowed her longing and took a deep breath in a vain attempt to clear her mind. It didn't work. She turned back to the terrain and kicked her horse into motion.

After long, silent moments, he spoke. "Tell me, Miss Bri."

"What, Mr. Morgan?"

"How'd you come about having such a good understanding of this area? Were your parents missionaries?"

"No. My father was a professor."

"Let me guess—he sent you off with a pair of missionaries to settle your spirit."

She flashed him a wry grin. "My parents died when I was nine."

"Oh. I'm sorry to hear that."

"It's water under the bridge."

"So, how is it that you know the back country so well?"

"Maps, Mr. Morgan. The Denver land office is filled with maps."

He frowned in puzzlement. "You mentioned maps before, but I never see you consult one."

"I do," she replied. "They're all up here." She tapped a gloved finger against her head.

"I don't understand."

"Neither do I really. But ever since I was small I

could remember precisely anything I saw or read, like maps or books."

"No one has a memory that good."

She shrugged. "I see the pictures in my head."

He felt a chill of dread. "So, you're telling me you've been barreling through the wilderness based on what you remember of the maps in your head?"

She didn't answer him.

He was dumbfounded, couldn't believe she'd be that stupid. "Well?" he demanded.

She still didn't answer him. By God, he wanted to strangle her. What gall, what arrogance, what stupidity. He didn't know anyone that brash, especially not a woman.

"You're nuts."

"No," she replied in that schoolmarm tone. "I'm well motivated."

"What could motivate a woman to be so rash?" He bellowed. "Someone holding your lover for ransom?"

She stiffened in her saddle and a dark dread itched down his skin.

"That's it? That's why you're risking your neck and mine?"

"You have no idea what you're talking about."

Then why had the feeling in his gut just gone sour? He glared at her back. It didn't make sense. She didn't handle herself like a femme fatal. No, if she did have a lover somewhere, she'd have used the usual female ways of getting money. Heck, with her looks and figure, she could have had any number of miners eating out of her hand. He knew two or three that would have given her anything she wanted just to say they had dinner with her.

She stopped suddenly, her face taking on a look of concern. The sun beat down on them; the hum of insects and birds filled the air. Everything seemed okay. Then he heard it, too—the sound that had made her stop—and the hairs on the back of his neck rose. The faint sound of human activity carried on the wind.

She turned the horses back and left their trail. With caution they climbed up the edge of the underridge. She stopped halfway and slid off her horse. She tossed him a glance telling him to stay put, but he'd already made up his mind to stay close to her, no matter what.

So he shook his head and slid off his horse. She frowned at him and pulled that infernal gun out of her holster; the look she shot him told him she'd use it if she had to.

He grinned at her and shook his head, then nodded back toward the sound. If she used the gun, she'd let the entire valley know they were there.

She huffed and put it away. He sauntered toward her. She pulled out the Bowie. He nodded her forward. They moved silent and steady to the highest point under the ridge and squatted out of sight. She studied the terrain until she stopped on a point to the right.

He followed the direction of her gaze. He could see the stream winding in and out of the pines along the mountainside. Then he made out one horse, two, five, twenty, and to the right of that, teepees, at least five.

They'd stumbled onto a band of renegades.

She moved and his gaze went to her. She sat back

on her heels and chewed on her bottom lip. Darn, but he wanted to chew on it too.

"We'll have to go back," he said low.

"Hmm," she replied. It sounded like a purr. He swallowed. Now was not the time or place to lose his head.

"Your maps didn't tell you about this," he said.

She shot him a dirty look and started drawing in the gravelly mountainside with the tip of the Bowie. "There's only one other pass close by," she said. Her voice was so low he had to lean in to hear her. She smelled of clean woman and mountain air. She glanced up at him and frowned, then continued to draw the mountain edge showing the stream and the ridge they now sat under. "It means going a day out of our way." She pointed out where they were and where the other pass was. They'd have to backtrack down the mountain and then go up and over another mountain to reach a southern pass.

That way would take them at least a day's travel into deep wilderness. She looked up at him, willing him to understand.

He understood all right. He understood that things were getting out of hand.

"Look." He kept his gaze on her, willing her to believe him. "This is crazy. I'm telling you I'm not worth it."

She snorted.

He grew more serious. "It would be smarter to backtrack a couple of days. We'll come up on my brothers. They'll straighten this out. I promise."

She stood up and slipped the knife effortlessly under his chin. "We ride."

He scowled at her. "I'll give you the thousand. I've got that and more."

"I don't take charity. Now, let's go."

He gritted his teeth in frustration. "You're a fool."

She nodded her agreement. "Perhaps. But, if I am, I'm a fool on a quest. Mount up."

He didn't have much choice. The knife in his back brought him back to the mare. He mounted. She slid the weapon back into place and with quick precision, hid their tracks.

Then once again she led them back down the mountain. This time they rode in determined silence. Both listened intently to see if they were discovered or followed, if they had managed to skirt around the encampment totally unnoticed. So far, it seemed that way.

By the time Brianna found the creek again, they'd traveled almost four hours without water. She thought she would die of thirst and knew the horses had to be hurting.

She got off and let her mount drink while she scouted for the best place to ford. Trey slipped down as well and nudged his mount toward the water.

He had an angry, dangerous look in his eye. The tiger was back. She swallowed the nervous emotions that erupted along her spine and reached for the gun.

"Put that thing away," he growled. "I'm not going to jump you."

"That's not what your expression is telling me." She let her hand rest on the handle. A flick of her thumb unfastened the holster cover. If she had to, she could withdraw it between one breath and the next, and they both knew it. For the moment, she pacified him and left it in the leather.

He rolled his eyes toward the heavens and took a deep breath. "Just because I want to strangle you, doesn't mean I will."

The words were a threat that made the hairs on the back of her neck stand on edge. The tiger had come to life.

"You're in no position to make threats," she pointed out. "I've got to do what I think is best to reach my goal. You're just along for the ride."

His eyes narrowed at her words. "I think I have more at stake here than you. This is my life we're talking about."

She opened her mouth but he cut her off before the words got out. "Don't tell me you could shoot me and be done with it. You're not killing anyone, especially since you've no proof I'm guilty of any crime."

She didn't like to admit it, but he was right. She had never had that option and they both knew it. Darn.

"Fine." She raised her chin high. "That doesn't mean I won't wound you if you try to run or hurt me in any way. I believe in self-defense."

"I'm certain you do," he said. "So let's talk about this turn of events."

She turned to the horses. They had had their fill and munched the tall grasses growing around the bank.

"There's nothing to talk about. We're halfway to the second pass."

He came up behind her. She whirled, gun in hand. There was no way she was letting him crowd her today. Too much was at stake, her brother Ethan being the number one thing.

"Back off," she said, letting some of her anger and frustration come through in her tone.

He stopped three feet from her. "This is nuts," he said through gritted teeth. "I told you, I have the money."

"I don't want your blood money."

"For God's sake, it's not blood money."

"I don't want pity," she said.

"Then what the hell do you want?"

"I want justice."

His eyes widened. "This is justice?" he turned enough to indicate his tied hands, the red welts that the cuffs had made over the past week.

She felt a shudder of guilt but pushed it away. "Yes, as best I can tell, it is justice," she replied without blinking. "I've got the wanted poster to prove it." She clung to the only evidence she had. That poster would be her brother's salvation. Even if it killed her.

"Is it worth your life as well as mine?" he asked with a softer tone.

She gave him her most solemn look. "It's worth it," she replied and she believed.

He sobered up, his gaze searching her expression. Then he nodded. "I have to trust that it is."

Relief washed over her. "Mount up, we have a lot of territory to cover if we want to camp by water tonight."

Trey knew he was in deep trouble. The minx had him following her against his better judgement. He couldn't help it. He was . . . irresistably intrigued. What was so important that she'd lay down her life for it? It was obvious that she'd rather lay down her life than flirt, coerce, or sell herself for it. She refused his money flat out, and he was certain she believed he'd give it to her.

He followed her lead over the rocky terrain without thought. Both he and his mount were conditioned to following. It was not a good sign. He'd kept alert for any sign that they might have picked up a trail from the Indian camp.

So far nothing was obvious. He glanced around. The wilderness stretched out before them, nothing but wooded mountainside that led to rocky cliffs and dangerous gullies.

Still she trudged on with little more than a compass and the sun. He'd been this way once or twice before when he wanted to lose sight of another man or when some idiot thought to hunt him down. As much as he hated to admit it, she had yet to get lost.

He glanced at her back. It was rigid as steel, with her hair in its simple long braid that hung down the middle. Her hat shielded her from the grueling sun and harsh wind.

Only the sounds of the wilderness filled his ears—insects, an occasional bird, and the sound of their horses climbing.

She was noble, intelligent, and stubborn as an ox. Perhaps it was time to bedevil her for a while. It was the only revenge he had.

"Don't you think it's time I got another shave?" he asked. He hadn't raised his voice, but the woods were so quiet that the sound bounced off the trees.

She didn't even flinch. "I think you need a bath more than you need a shave, Mr. Morgan."

"Why do you say that?" He whiffed his armpit. "Nothing but healthy man."

"Cleanliness is next to godliness, Mr. Morgan."

"Really, is that why you're so high-handed?" The light jab did not even budge her back. He frowned until a thought crossed his mind. "You going to bath me, Teach?"

She rode on for two whole strides before she answered. "I think you're old enough to get the job done yourself."

"With my hands tied behind me? It's going to be a bit of a stretch."

"I'm sure we'll think of something."

His grin widened. He could think of a lot of different ways to get the job done.

Chapter Seven

"This is the place." Brianna looked down on the small stream that wound over the side of the mountain. It had been a long, hard ride, and she felt like she had an inch of dusty grit all over. When she spoke, dust ground against her teeth.

She glanced at her captive. He looked none the worse for wear, even covered with dust and stubble.

They were pretty deep into the backcountry. It made her nervous. The maps didn't have a whole lot to say about this area, so she felt vulnerable. Trey's anger and distress over her choice didn't help, either. She eyed the surrounding terrain. Nothing seemed amiss so she shrugged the feeling off.

It was probably Trey's fault anyway. If he hadn't been so adamant against this route, she would feel more confident. It was the last time she would let him know where she was taking him. Besides, he was probably just upset because those wonderful brothers of his hadn't caught up to them yet, and this new twist in direction just might shake them.

It was a small comfort.

She eased the horses down toward the stream. There was a nice campsite halfway between a bluff that overlooked the water and the actual water. The bluff would be too exposed to camp on, but the level spot between was perfect.

"This is it," she said and slid down. When she hit the ground, her whole body jerked with pain. She ignored it. After weeks on horseback, she'd managed to work through the worst of the pain. She smiled. She had become one tough old bird.

She busied herself caring for the horses while Trey scrutinized the site. "Does it meet your approval?"

"It'll do."

"Good," she said. "Let's go."

He raised an eyebrow in a silent question.

"Bath time."

"How?" He rolled his shoulders and emphasized his cuffed hands.

"A little soap, some icy water. It'll come back to you." She pulled out the gun and waved it forward. "After you."

He complied without another word. She wondered what he was thinking, then decided she really didn't want to know.

She stopped him before he reached the edge of the stream.

"Hold on." It was an instant decision, one borne out

of pity. The man's hands had been tied the entire journey. It was time to see if she could trust him enough to wash himself or if she'd have to wound him a little.

He stopped in midstride. She pulled out her knife and touched his back. "I'm going to take these cuffs off, but I still have my weapons. Don't try—"

"Anything." He finished for her.

"Right." She pulled out the key to the handcuffs. With a click, they fell into her hand. He did not move. Her heart raced with anticipation. It was times like this when she was most vulnerable and they both knew it.

"Don't use all the hot water," she said sarcastically.

He slowly raised his hands over his head and took two strides away. She took the time to scramble up to the edge of the bluff. "You can put your hands down now, Mr. Morgan. I've got you covered. You won't get far."

He turned and she cocked the gun in her hand. "Soap?" She tossed it down to him. He caught it with ease. Even after all the days of being tied, his reflexes were quick. Something sent a warning down her spine. The tiger was still not subdued, and it was best she not forget it.

"Thanks." He pulled off his shirt and socks. He didn't wear a union suit under his clothes so his wide shoulders and strong muscled back were bare and tanned under the setting sun.

The view took her breath away. Then he did the unimaginable. He stripped off his pants. She inhaled sharply. He glanced over his shoulder to see if she still had her eye on him. She swallowed.

"Time's awastin' " she hollered. It was the best she could do—that, and fight the blush that threatened to give her away. He turned his head back to the stream and strode in.

She sat down cross-legged on the edge of the bluff. Her knees had somehow turned to jam and refused to hold her up. The man was magnificent and completely tanned all over, which meant he was no stranger to bathing in the wilderness.

She took several deep breaths in a sad attempt to still her racing heart and cool her blood. Why, oh, why couldn't he have been short, fat, and ugly?

She scanned the surrounding area and knew there was no answer to her question—no answer to this awful attraction she had to this man. He was more attractive than Arthur's Lancelot. More real than the statues of the Greek and Roman gods that were scattered around the Wilmington's Boston garden.

She took another deep breath and inhaled cool dusk air. It smelled of sun-warmed earth, wild plants, and just a hint of snow.

Her gaze swept over him as he ducked under, then resurfaced and lathered up. Okay, so she wasn't as cool as she'd hoped she could be, but darn, he was easy on her eyes.

He lathered his long dark hair as best he could with the lye soap, then rinsed it in the stream. Fascinated with his every movement, she rested the pistol in her lap. The sound of humming insects and calling birds filled the air with life.

Good lord, she was tired. It felt good just to sit and

listen to the stillness of the earth. As the shadows lengthened, she had the sudden thought that she could stay here and watch him for the rest of her life and never tire of the view.

A sound from behind her sent shock waves through her body and she became as still as a rabbit in the grass. She listened intently but didn't turn. She didn't want to call attention to herself.

The sound came again. There was the snap of a twig, and the birds fell silent. Even the insects stopped. The air stilled as if every creature held its breath.

She inched her hand toward the gun in her lap.

"Don't move!" The words floated on the air. Fully aware of danger behind her, her gaze went to the naked man standing waist deep in the stream. The words were his, not shouted but called calmly as if he'd told her they were having roast for Sunday dinner.

She could tell from the look in his eyes that he knew exactly what the danger was and, God help her, she was going to have to trust him to see her through.

She glanced down at the gun in her lap and then back up at him. He shook his head using the barest of movements.

It was as if time had stopped. She was aware of something over her shoulder, something big. She could almost feel it breathing. No one moved. She barely breathed while her mind raced over different scenarios. She could grab the gun, turn and shoot, and hope that whatever it was was exactly where she thought it was.

If she were quick enough she could turn, shoot, and grab her knife in case the bullets missed.

There was little Trey could do. She had all the weapons. What he had was knowledge of the particulars—and she wished he were kind enough to share.

A slight breeze rustled up and she heard him, faint like a birdcall, calm and unexpected. "Big cat. Three feet left."

She took a slow easy breath. Okay, so it was a cat, a very big cat. Thoughts of her aunt's housecats came to mind. She remembered how they would stalk a mouse, then crouch and watch the terrified creature until they'd had enough. Then they would pounce, claw, and bite.

Her neck hurt from the image. She was so tuned in to the animal she swore she could hear its heart beating. She looked back down at the gun. It was her only choice. On the count of three she would grab, turn, and shoot.

One . . . Two . . . Three—

"No!"

She grabbed the gun, simultaneously turned, and cocked it with her left hand. The cat was huge. Its golden eyes were mere inches above her as it leaped. She squeezed the trigger, cocked the hammer, squeezed the trigger. It took three shots before the cat was on her.

Its breath was hot and smelled wild. Claws ripped her shoulder and arm, knocking the gun from her hand. Acting instinctively, everything slow and cold as her heartbeat, she kicked, shoving the heavy cat.

The cat jumped back, landed on its feet and stared at her, but did not move.

She scrambled away. She knew that if the cat struck again, she would die. Bri had her small knife in her hand. If she were going to die, she would take the cat with her. Suddenly Trey was across from her. He motioned for her not to move.

She felt frozen but managed to indicate with her eyes that she understood. It was then that she noticed the Bowie knife in his hand. He leaped like a wild man and was on the animal between one heartbeat and the next. Blood surged as he slit the cat's throat.

Bri sank to the ground. It was over. A flood of relief filled her, drowning her exhausted body. Blackness settled over her eyes, bringing a peace that she hadn't known since the days before her parents died.

Trey stood, knife in hand. His heart raced in his chest. He hadn't been that afraid in a long, long time. He glanced at the cat. It was the biggest mountain lion he'd ever seen. A female most likely hunting food for her cubs. He brushed his wet hair out of his eyes and glanced over to see if Bri was all right.

She had crumpled like a bundle of clothes. "Shoot." He moved to put the knife in his waistband and realized he was stark naked. He'd remedy that later. Right now he needed to make sure she was all right.

He was to her in two strides. He hunkered down and rolled her over. She was pale from shock. Long red angry gouges ran down her left shoulder where the cat had attacked.

He needed to get her cleaned up. He tucked the knife between his teeth and picked her up. She was light as a feather and endearingly vulnerable in his arms. Blood seeped out of her wounds. He knew some blood was necessary to clean away any poison from the cat's claws, but too much and she would die.

He took her down to the river where he removed her jacket and shirt. Her skin was pale as cream under her clothing and soft as the underbelly of a calf.

The wounds were deep. He scrambled to tear pieces of his shirt into bandages. He washed the cuts as best he could, then pressed the cloth on them until the blood stopped.

He held her in his arms. Her beautiful face rested against his bare chest as trustingly as a babe's, and he felt anger welling up deep inside him.

What the heck was she doing a million miles from nowhere, dragging no-good criminals to justice? Was he her only catch? Had there been others? There couldn't have been; she was too exhausted from this relentless pushing.

What she needed was rest, fresh meat, and a man to take care of her. Someone had to look after her. She sure as heck wasn't looking after herself.

He folded her jacket and used it as a pillow for her head. Then he pulled his pants on, grabbed a gun and his Bowie knife, which he'd snagged on his way up the hill, and went to make sure there weren't any other surprises hiding around their campsite. They were camping here for the night; she needed the rest and he wasn't taking no for an answer.

He scouted a hundred-yard distance around. The cat had left scratches high in a big pine, a sign that this was her territory. He found no evidence of a den or cubs, but it would be something they'd have to keep an eye on. The horses didn't seem at all bothered by the danger that had passed so close. He frowned at that. The cat hadn't been stalking them. If that were the case, it would have gone after the horses first. No, it must have been on the bluff the moment she scrambled up there with the gun. It was just watching and waiting for its moment to attack.

Emotion twined down his spine, causing him to curse under his breath. He'd been helpless standing naked and weaponless in the stream. All he could do was remain calm and pray she wouldn't do anything stupid.

He finished the check of the perimeter and headed back into camp. There were no signs of Indians or anymore predators, but that didn't mean they weren't there. From now on, he was in charge of this little expedition and, after they had a decent meal, he was going to find out just what the heck she thought she was doing.

Bri had a tremendous headache and her mouth felt like it was filled with old musty cotton. She hadn't felt this bad since she was thirteen and Billy Manson had dared her to drink three shots of moonshine.

She tried to sit up, but her shoulder ached so bad it was better just to stay put and keep her eyes shut.

"Drink," came a non-too-gentle order. She felt an

arm go around her shoulders and lift her. She wanted to protest at the pain, but the moment she opened her mouth, water was poured in. She sputtered, then drank a bit, hoping her torturer would soon decide she'd had enough and put her back down on the lovely ground.

The water never stopped. She finally turned her head. "Enough." The water stopped and she was put back down. "Ouch!" She raised her hand to her forehead.

"Sorry," came the very male reply, not sounding all that contrite. She tried to place him. The realization of just who he was shattered through the haze of pain, and her eyes flew wide open.

Trey Morgan moved back to a small fire and hunkered down beside it. Something smelled wonderful. No—on second whiff it smelled nasty. She struggled to sit up, but the pain made her nauseated, and she lost what little she had eaten that day.

He was beside her again, and canteen in hand, he wet down her handkerchief. "Here, lay back down and put this on your forehead."

She grimaced and did what he ordered. Her heart raced and her head pounded, but mostly her shoulder ached as if she'd run it through a sausage grinder. She knew she was in deep danger. The balance of power had shifted. The tiger she'd had by the tail now stood over her and if she weren't careful he could devour her in one sitting.

She had no clue what to do now. She had to do something. Her brother, Ethan, still needed her. Mr. Fry's book said that sometimes the best thing to do was to play dead. This seemed like a good time to do just that. Perhaps if he thought she was hurt really bad he'd underestimate her and give her a chance to regain the upper hand.

"Can I die now?" she whispered.

"Some fresh meat will help you feel better." She peeked at him from under her lashes. He wore only his pants, leaving his chest bare to the cool night air.

If her body didn't ache so bad she might even have enjoyed the view. The man was all muscle with a sprinkling of soft black hair down the middle.

"No, no meat," she managed to croak out. "The smell turns my stomach."

"That's because you're shocky from the attack."

Her eyes popped open as a thought entered her head. It was a strange and terrible thought. Not at all reasonable, but then he didn't really look like a reasonable man. No, right now he looked very much like the ruthless killer in the wanted poster.

"What kind of meat is it?"

"Fresh."

She swallowed hard. "Fresh what?"

"Fresh rabbit."

She let her breath out. Her stomach felt a bit better. Cat was not on the menu. The thought made her stomach roll.

"I made beans, too, but you need the meat. You've lost a lot of blood." He dumped beans and meat on a tin plate and brought it to her. "Eat."

She took the plate. It actually looked good. He handed her a spoon, but she couldn't move her other arm. She struggled to reach, but it caused too much pain.

"Here," he said, not sounding very happy. He took the plate and filled the spoon and fed her. "Eat."

She took a bite. It tasted very good. She chewed slowly, letting the food ease into her stomach. He shoved another spoonful up to her face. It was oddly intimate having him feed her, but she didn't have much choice. Now he was in the position of power.

It struck her that he would probably just wait here until his brothers showed up. She couldn't let that happen. She couldn't let the brothers find them, or there wouldn't be any bounty. No bounty. No help for her little brother.

"My shoulder really hurts. What happened?"

"The cat mauled you pretty good before it went down."

She refused another bite. "I don't feel too well."

He frowned and set the plate aside, then eased her back down. She rested her head on her saddle, and he tucked a blanket in around her. "The cuts are pretty deep."

"Do you think I need a doctor?"

"Probably," he admitted.

"There's a doctor in Durango."

"It will be easier when my brothers get here."

Panic filled her. "I don't think it should wait. I feel awfully warm." It wasn't entirely a lie. She felt on the edge of feverish.

He put a hand to her forehead and his frown deepened. "Infection might be setting in."

"Then you have to get me to a doctor," she begged. "We're only three and a half days away from town. Please don't let me die out here." She gave him her best "wounded" look. He might be a hardened criminal, but her friends had said her looks could melt a heart of stone. It was her only chance.

His frown deepened just as a shiver overtook her. "Did I say I was hot?" she asked. "Because I lied. I'm cold, tired and cold." She closed her eyes. She was suddenly exhausted. The trip had been so long . . . and she had given it her best shot.

Three and a half days. She had come so close. All she could do now was wait and see if her plea had melted his criminal heart.

Trey tossed another blanket on top of her and cursed the sky above. She had gotten to him. After kidnapping him and dragging him across the mountains, all she had to do was look at him and he turned to mush.

He ground his teeth. He was a sap, that's what he was. A big ball of mush at the beck and call of a pair of angel eyes. Shoot.

As much as he might want to, he couldn't let her die. She was so darned soft and vulnerable, a huge puzzle he still wanted—no, needed—to figure out. Why had she kidnapped him? What was so important that she would risk her life to bring him in? Money? Money had been all Katherine was after. He reminded himself that he had sworn off women. Sworn never to let one into his heart.

He glanced down at the woman shivering at the

edge of his campfire. Her teeth chattered, but she slept. It was a feverish sleep. She needed him. Even now when he finally had control, he was at her mercy.

He banked the fire and grabbed his blanket. She was right. He couldn't let her die. He lay down beside her and pulled her against him. She was hot. As hot as the fire on the other side of him. He grimaced and tucked her in beside him.

She wrapped her arm around him and put her head on his shoulder. "You smell nice," she said.

He glanced down but she didn't open her eyes. "So do you," he said, and pulled his blanket over the two of them. The heat from her body had him sweating in a minute, but he knew she was the one who needed to sweat.

"I wish you were mine," she said and shivered hard.

Panic went through him first, followed by a warmth he didn't think he would ever feel again. He pulled her against him and she stopped shaking. She rested her head against his shoulder like a tiny babe.

He sighed deeply and kissed her heated temple. "I wish the same," he admitted to the cold night air. "I wish the same."

He settled down for what he knew would be a very long, very hard night.

Chapter Eight

The next night Trey got up to stir the fire. Bri had finally quieted and the worst of the fever was over. He stretched and got some water from his canteen. She had been so hot and so close that he felt like he had sweated out half his body weight.

He felt some relief when the fever had finally broken. She was going to live.

He wasn't sure if he was or not.

Something had happened during those long hours when he'd held her close. Her body had imprinted itself on his; her breath had mingled with his. And he swore she had stolen a piece of his soul.

Somewhere between the time she kidnapped him and the last ten minutes, he had lost his heart.

Why? What was it? Sure she was beautiful, but he'd had his share of beautiful women. Katherine had probably been prettier, in the fashionable sense. Maybe it was Bri's grit and determination. It was as if the hounds of hell chased her and she refused to let them get her.

Or maybe it was her vulnerability. She seemed to know exactly where she was going; yet it was clear she hadn't spent much time in the wilderness.

That's it. She was a puzzle—a mystery so complex it could take a man a lifetime to figure it out.

He glanced at her lying under the blankets, her face flush with fever and sleep. She smelled like his. She felt like his. It set off warning bells deep within him.

He knew he couldn't trust her. Experience had taught him that. He suspected she would turn on him the moment she had a chance. But something inside him didn't want to hear the warning. He mentally shrugged it off.

When she woke up, he'd nurse her back to health. Then he'd take her to Durango and find out what it was that was so important she'd risk her life and limb for it. Money was the obvious answer, but he couldn't accept that. It had to be more. He took another swig of the cold water. Time would tell.

A twig snapped, off to the right of camp. Trey's gun was in his hand before he finished taking a breath. "Come out where I can see you," he said, low and threatening. "I can do a lot of killing just by guessing."

The noise grew as two men emerged from the dark.

"Dagnab it, Trey, you'd think we were outlaws or something," Taggart grumbled. "I figured you'd have known your own kin by our scent."

"We don't smell pretty," Matt said. "Tag worse than me, of course."

Trey shook his head as the two men pushed each other around and argued over who had the worst stench. He realized that during those years he'd spent alone he had missed his brothers. Family had somehow become important to him. Even if it meant listening to his brothers argue.

With relief he put his gun back in its holster. "What took you so long?"

"What took us so long? Heck, the trail was as convoluted as an Indian trail. When it wasn't, you were moving so fast we figured you were peeing in your drawers."

"Sounds to me like you two have gotten soft," Trey said.

"Soft, heck, I haven't seen backtracking like that since old Grayfeather died." Tag threw his gear down next to the fire and sat down. "You got any coffee?"

"There's a pot set up to boil." Trey said and pointed at the tin coffeepot next to the flames. "Put it on if you want some."

Matt put his gear down and stretched. He glanced around and spied Bri. "Who's that?"

"Her name is Bri."

"What happened?"

Trey squatted down and poked at the fire. "It's a long story."

"Is she okay?" Tag asked. "She looks bad."

"We had a run-in with a big cat."

"You get hurt?" Matt asked. "You certainly don't look any worse for wear."

"I'm fine," he said. "She's pretty banged up."

"Okay, so what happened?" Tag asked. "Who dragged you this far and how did you get away? Did they kidnap the girl too?"

Trey played with the fire. He felt protective of Bri and wasn't sure how his brothers would feel about the truth.

"Trey?" Matt asked. "I don't see any evidence of a big scuffle."

"There wasn't one."

"Then what happened?" Matt asked.

"Yeah, why are we nearly in Nevada?" Tag asked.

Trey was silent a moment. "Bri's a bounty hunter."

"What?!" The two men spoke at once.

"There is no way she could be a bounty hunter," Tag declared.

"Yeah, that's what I said when she arrested me," Trey said. "Seems she saw that wanted poster you had made up. The one that got me arrested long enough for you to find me and tell me Ma had died and the ranch was mine."

"It was meant to hold you, not kill you," Matt said. "Besides, I paid the bounty and made sure everyone knew it."

"She didn't know it."

"Well, did she ask?"

"No, she just took it upon herself to arrest me and take me back."

"What would a gal like her want with bounty hunting?" Matt asked.

"The money, I suppose," Trey replied.

"I ain't believin' it. You're puttin' me on." Tag jumped to his feet. "Ain't no way that little bitty slip of a girl got you this far by herself." Tag pulled out his gun and looked around. "Where's the rest of the gang?"

"There is no gang."

"That's what they want you to say, right? It's a trap, isn't it?"

Trey stood and pushed his brother's gun until it pointed toward the ground. "Put it away. There isn't anyone else here."

Tag narrowed his eyes. "Swear on Ma's grave."

"I swear on Ma's grave there isn't anyone but her. Now put your gun away."

"How'd she do it?" Matt asked.

Trey looked over to see Matt lounging by the fire. He'd taken off his jacket and settled in for the night. It was clear he was surprised, but not shocked by her behavior.

"Got me," Trey said. "She's got some kind of map in her head. She acts like she knows exactly where we're going, but I swear she doesn't know too much about the actual terrain."

"She a city girl?" Matt asked.

Trey looked at Tag. He stood in the same spot frowning at Bri. "Best I can tell," Trey said. "She sounds educated. Tag, relax, there isn't anyone going to come out of the bushes."

Matt poured himself a cup of coffee. "Women. They're the darndest creatures. I swear I'd have never thought they could do half the stuff Samantha does, but then she just goes and does it."

Trey picked up his canteen and wetted his bandana; then he placed it on Bri's forehead. She was sweating heavily now. The worst of the fever was over.

"I can't believe that little slip of nothing bested you," Tag said. He still stood by the fire staring.

Trey shrugged. He didn't feel ashamed. He'd seen her in action and he knew how wiley she could be. She'd have danced circles around his brothers. He reached down and caressed her cheek.

The sky lightened and he knew morning was coming. The pinks of first light turned her skin the color of a rich pearl. He wondered what it would be like to see that color every morning for the rest of his life.

"You're telling me that we couldn't track some slip of a girl? That I haven't slept more than four hours a night for weeks because you let some girl haul you through high country?" Tag took a step toward him. "What were you thinkin'? Or were you even thinkin'? Why didn't you leave us some kind of sign to go home? Or was she so good you didn't even think about those of us with lives?"

Anger rushed through Trey, anger so deep it rocked him. He surged to his feet and planted his fist in Tag's nose. His brother went down.

"That's enough," Matt said. His tone was loud and firm enough to push through Trey's emotion. Trey looked down to see his Bowie knife in his hand. He took a deep breath and sheathed it.

Tag held his nose. Blood dripped down the side of his hand. He frowned. "What's the matter with you? I thought you hated women."

Trey retreated to the disappearing shadows. He had to get a hold of himself. He took another deep breath. He did hate women—but not all women.

He glanced at Bri. She slept now. It was the quiet peaceful sleep of rest. She looked so vulnerable. Yet he knew she was smart, savvy, and could be as tough as nails. He couldn't hate her. Not when he'd have admired those qualities in a man.

Trey heard Matt get up and come over. His brother put his hand on his shoulder. "You okay?"

"Fine."

"She got to you didn't she?"

"She's different."

"Yeah," Matt said. "If she did what you said she did, then I'd say she was different. I'd say she was downright gifted."

Trey looked at his brother with narrowed eyes. Matt backed off and put his hands in the air. "I wasn't im-plying anything. Really. I just figure she'd have to have talent to get you this far and keep us at bay."

Trey relaxed. "Yeah. She surprised me."

"Is she okay?"

"She had a brawl with the biggest damned mountain lion I'd ever seen."

Matt glanced at her. "And she lived?"

"Pumped the cat with three shots and had a knife in her hand before I could get to her."

"Wow."

"It mauled her pretty good. Her shoulder and arm are going to be scarred, but the fever broke, so I think she'll survive."

"What are you going to do with her?"

"Get her well enough to escort her to Durango. I'm curious to see what happens when she finds out the bounty's been paid."

"What do you want us to do?"

"Go home. I can handle this."

"I'm sure you can," Matt said. "Just make sure you come home. Otherwise Tag will turn the ranch into a horse farm."

Trey grimaced at the thought. But Matt was right. If Trey were to leave again, the ranch would go to Tag. Tag was the best horseman around, but he knew darned little about cattle.

"I'll be back."

"Just don't make me post another wanted poster," Matt said. "The last one got you into this kind of trouble. Imagine if some idiot thought they could kill you."

"They'd be dead before they had another thought," Trey said.

"And you'd be in jail for real. Don't do it. I like having you around."

Trey looked into his brother's eyes and saw that he spoke the truth. There was a bond there that would never be broken. After all, his brothers had left their work, Matt had even left his new wife to come chase after him. They knew he'd do the same for them.

"You guys get some coffee and food in you, get some rest, then head back home." Matt turned to do just that when Trey stopped him. "You didn't by chance happen to bring my boots, did you?"

Matt glanced at Trey's feet and grinned. "Naw, Tag said you were tough enough to walk back without them."

"That boy owes me."

Matt's grin widened. "Yeah. He'll get his. I figure he's gotta be next."

Brianna had the strangest dream. It was warm and romantic. She had lain all night in her lover's arms, while he cradled her and caressed her hair and whispered how much he loved her. It was a sweet dream. One she had had when she was younger, but had put away when her parents died.

After all, who would want a single mother, and that was what she would be as soon as she got Ethan back. By the time the boy was old enough to go to university, Bri would be twenty-nine, far too old to attract suitors.

But in the meantime, the dream was something to be savored. She rubbed her cheek along the firm contours of his bare chest. His skin was warm and unexpectedly soft. There was fine hair that ran along the top of contoured muscle. She touched his chest, relishing the shape and textures. He was pure muscle underneath. Rather like the Greek statues she had observed, only he was warm and alive, not cold like the stone had been.

"Honey, you better keep your hands to yourself or we're going to be in a heap of trouble."

Brianna opened her eyes at the sound of a distinctly male voice. She inhaled sharply and understood that her imagination was not nearly as good as the scent of him.

Shock went through her. She rose up in a rush only to find that the pain from her actions brought her just as quickly back down into the man's arms. "Ugh."

He wrapped his arms around her and cradled her. "It's okay," he said softly. "I won't hurt you."

She ground her teeth as pain pulsed through her arm. "Jeez, why didn't you just slit my throat and be done with it?"

He chuckled. The sound was low and soft and vibrated through his chest. It was nice in an odd sort of way. He gently pushed her head back down on his chest. The motion was comforting. Like when her pa used to hold her when she had a bad dream.

"It's not that bad."

"That's what you say," she said and closed her eyes against the ache. He chuckled again and the vibration in his chest made her smile.

"I can get you some whiskey to take the edge off."

"You'd do that for me?"

He carefully rolled her off him and got out of the blankets. The loss of his heat brought a chill to her skin. She huddled deeper into the blankets. It was then that she realized she was wearing her shift. The thin cotton dress was the only thing between her and the world, and she had to pee.

She struggled to gather the blanket around her and sit up. The pain nearly knocked her back down, but her insistent bladder had other ideas.

"Lay down, I'll take care of you."

"No," she said and struggled to stand.

He was over to her in a flash with his hands around her shoulders. She reached up with her good arm to knock him away but could only grab the falling blanket.

"I said lay down, you're too weak to stand."

"You don't understand," she said. She met his gaze as clearly as she could. "It's necessary that I find a bush or something."

"Oh. Well, heck, I'd have figured you wouldn't have to go, what with the amount of sweat that's poured through you the last few days."

"The last few days?" she echoed. A creeping feeling of dread edged around her mind.

"After the cat mauled you, I cleaned you up the best I could. Fever set in and you've been down for about three days."

"Three days." She fell against him as her knees buckled slightly. Three days. What day would this be? Did she miss the deadline she had set? Did Ethan think she had abandoned him? "What day is this?"

"Thursday."

She did some quick calculations in her head. It was okay; She still had a week. "Where are we?"

He looked at her with concern. "We're still at the camp where the mountain lion jumped you."

So they were a good three and a half days out of town.

"Why?" he asked.

"I don't like missing time," she replied blithely. "Now, please, I have to do the necessary." She gathered the blanket around her and strode off as gracefully as she could into the woods.

"Don't go far. I think I saw bear tracks this morning."

His warning caused a shiver of fear to brush down her back. She glanced all around before finding an appropriate bush. The last time she had been lax, the mountain lion had gotten her. Now she hurt like crazy and all her careful plans had been turned upside down.

It was clear he hadn't taken her to town, but also clear that he had nursed her during the worst.

What was a cold-blooded murderer doing taking care of her and her wounds? Especially after she had arrested him and threatened to kill him. Curious.

She finished up and gathered the blanket back around her. The woods were dimming. It had to be late afternoon already. If she were going to make her deadline, they needed to be on the road tomorrow.

Anxious to see what kind of shape she was in, she moved her shoulder. The motion made her gasp.

"You okay?"

His voice was so close she jumped out of her skin and nearly dropped the blanket. The action sent another round of agony shooting through her shoulder.

"Yeah, I'm just fine," she said through her teeth and marched to the fire. When she arrived she sat down. She was exhausted. Just a trip out to do her business had left her drained. And her arm . . . well, she was going to take a good look at it now.

"Here's that whiskey," he said, handing her a bottle. She took it.

"Do you really think I'm going to need it?"

He hunkered down beside her. "Take a swig. I need to remove your bandage and clean your wounds." He glanced at her. His eyes were now cobalt blue and mesmerizing. "I won't lie to you. You're going to need the whiskey."

She took a swig from the bottle; her gaze never left his eyes. As the cold glass edge of the bottle touched her lips, she found herself dangerously close to some unknown emotion. It was a vague yet thrilling one. And his eyes led her to it.

"Drink."

She did as ordered and took a long swig. The liquid hit the back of her throat and burned. Her eyes watered and all the air rushed out of her lungs, but she refused to let on. "Not bad," she said when she could talk.

"Take another drink."

It was an alarming order. She could already feel the effects in her stomach. The whiskey spread like a slow burn, warming her insides and causing her face to flush. He looked at her as if to demand that she trust him.

Her armed throbbed, and she decided she didn't

have a choice. She put the bottle to her lips again and swallowed four gulps.

This time it tasted better, like oak and earth and maybe even grain. The burning was less pronounced. Probably because she had already burned away any feeling she had in her throat and stomach. But she had to admit the pain was definitely dulled.

"Good," he said and took the bottle from her. "Now, I'm going to unwrap the bandage and see what we have."

He pulled the blanket down off her arm and carefully rewrapped the rest of her. His movements were slow and filled with concern. She blinked. Her head was fuzzy and she distinctly felt the blood rushing through her heart and into her ears. For a brief moment, his hands were that of the lover in her dream. Caressing and gentle, they made her burn.

He untied the bandage and started to uncoil it from her shoulder and down her arm. She needed something to distract her.

"Why didn't you leave?" she asked.

"What?" He never looked up. Instead he concentrated on the bandage.

"Why didn't you leave? I mean, I meant to turn you in. You should have left the moment you were free."

"You begged me to stay."

"I did?"

"Umm hmm, you asked me not to let you die."

She bit her lip. He had to tug the last bit of bandage off. It was stuck to her oozing skin. The tug brought a fresh wave of torment and her head swam.

"Are you going to be sick?" he asked sharply.

She got a hold of herself. "Of course not," she said, swallowing hard. She looked down at the shredded skin on her shoulder and the deep wounds on her arm. "Are those stitches?" she squeaked.

"It will help lessen the scarring."

"I'm going to have scars?"

"Your wounds were pretty deep." He glanced up. "I did the best I could."

She swallowed her fear. He was right. He did the best he could. What did it matter if she could never wear an off–the–shoulder party dress again? She wasn't going to be going to too many parties. It wasn't like there'd ever be another man touching her bare skin.

"Well," she managed to squeak out. She studied the knots. "You did a very neat job."

"Ma taught us all to sew. She said, the rate we were going there would never be another woman in the house, and she wanted to make sure we could handle things on our own."

"Your mother was an intelligent woman."

He glanced at her. "She was a very brave woman. When she came to Wyoming, she was the only white woman for a hundred miles."

"What did she do for company?"

"She built her life around Pa and us boys."

"Family is important," Bri said. She couldn't keep the angst from her tone. "Without family we're nothing."

"Where's your family? You got a mister out there somewhere?"

The heat of a blush rushed up to her cheeks. The whiskey had her head spinning and she didn't have proper control of her emotions. "Goodness, no," she said swiftly. "Who would marry the likes of me?"

He tied on the new bandage and sat back on his heels. "What do you mean by that?"

"My pa always said I have more brains than sense. What man wants a woman like that?"

He stood. She watched him rise up. His chest was still bare, his pants wrinkled and dusty from wear and his feet were as naked as his chest.

She had a sudden flashback of him strolling into the stream, his golden skin all warm and alive, the sun glinting off his hair—and she wondered if she would ever see him that way again.

"I suppose your pa is right. Only a fool would want to straddle himself with a woman like that."

She reached for the whiskey bottle and took a couple more sips. Something inside her hurt; it wasn't her wound but something deeper. It was almost as if she had wanted to hear him say *he* would want a woman like her. She was truly insane. The man was wanted for murder. Wasn't he?

Trey snatched the bottle from her after two more swigs. "I'll take that. Trust me, you'll want to save some for later."

She took a deep breath. Suddenly the world began to spin. "I think I need to go lay down," she said. She tried to stand, but it was tough going. The farther she got from the ground, the more the air spun.

He lifted her in his arms and carried her over to the

bedroll. Then he slid her in and tucked the blanket around her.

"You know," she said and touched her hand to his beard-roughened cheek. "You aren't anything like I thought you'd be."

"What'd you think I'd be?" He asked.

She shrugged and closed her eyes. "I don't know, meaner, nastier—oh, and you'd smell bad." She smiled against the closing darkness. "But you smell real nice."

He took her hand and pulled it off his cheek. She opened her eyes to see him kiss her fingertips. "You're nothing like any bounty hunter I've ever met."

"Thank you," she said and hiccuped. "I think I'll take that as a compliment."

He pulled the blanket in tight. "Get some rest."

"Okay," she said and closed her eyes. "We're leaving in the morning," she announced.

"We are?"

"Oh, yes, Durango is a good four days away and I only have six days left to get back."

"What happens in six days?"

She smiled and turned onto her good side. "That's none of your business."

Chapter Nine

"Why didn't you leave?"

Her question from earlier rang through his head. He knew his brothers wondered the same thing. He supposed he could have had Matt or Tag take her to town and get rid of the poster, but the truth was, the idea of leaving her alone with anyone else bothered him.

Trey banked the fire and went through their pack. Bri was becoming more of a mystery every day. He figured tomorrow would be no different. He knew she was in no shape to travel, but he also had never seen a more stubborn woman in his life. So, he knew they'd be on the trail come morning. The question was, why?

He glanced at her. She slept like a child. Her hair was coming out of its moorings and tangled with the blankets. It was rich, dark stuff, smooth and shiny as silk. He had taken it into his hand as she slept, enjoyed the feel of it between his fingers, smelled it. It smelled of mountains, clean air, and woman.

It was the best scent he'd ever encountered, more real than the flowered fragrances of Katherine's hair. He had sworn he was over the hurt from Katherine, but now he knew different. He knew he had closed off his heart to all women because of her. He had closed his heart to ever having a family of his own, to avoid the pain of losing his child. It was time to change that—time to take back the parts of his soul he had let her kill.

He was no longer content with being a part of his brother's family. No, he wanted a family of his own. But his emotions were rusty. Bri had shown him there was still something there. When she curled up into his heat at night, she placed her cheek on his shoulder and her hand on his heart. It was enough to break off the tarnish, ease into the tattered remains of his heart.

He shook his head and prepared the packs for leaving. Deep inside there was the fear that she would betray him. Of course she would betray him. The question was why? Would there be a good reason? And if the reason was good enough, would he be able to accept it?

He doubted it.

He eased himself into the blankets beside her. She turned to him, her eyes closed, but a small smile played along the edges of her soft mouth. Her hand came to rest over his heart, and again he knew he was in deep.

Bri said the camp was four days from Durango.

That meant he had four days to woo her and to find out the answer to her mysteries. Would she really betray him? If so, why?

While she snuggled up next to him, every fiber of his being claimed her. Even though he knew she was destined to hurt him yet again. It was too late. She had stolen his heart when she stole him.

They rode hard the next day. Brianna hurt so badly, her teeth felt like they were permanently clenched. She did not complain. How could she? They were hurrying because she had demanded it and he had complied.

It was an awkward situation. She was no longer in control, yet he let her navigate their trail. He even let her pick the stopping place, catering to her wishes. Why?

It was as if he trusted her.

She led them to a decent campsite near a stream and let herself down off her horse with a grimace. "We made good time," she said. Talking distracted her from the pain.

He was beside her in an instant, quiet yet sure. He prepared her horse for the evening. She hadn't even had to ask. He just took over. His big hands made short work of the saddle and blankets. She walked in a small tight circle to stretch her legs and get some circulation back into her backside. Her shoulder throbbed. She had a feeling that if she sat down, she wouldn't get back up.

"I think I'll gather some wood for a small fire," she said.

"Don't go out of shouting range," he said. "No telling what's out here—bear, cat, Indian."

"Yes, well, no different than before," she said as blithely as possible and moved off into a small stand of trees. She slowly stretched, then bent to pick up manageable pieces of wood.

What she really needed was some time alone, time to think about what had happened over the course of her illness. It seemed Trey had moved into her bed out of necessity, but then he hadn't moved back out. It was disconcerting to wake up and find herself hauled up to his side. He held her tight as her brother held his teddy.

The man is a killer, she reminded herself. He's wanted by the law. She sighed and stared at the ground. She didn't believe the story he'd told her but her heart wasn't accepting the fact that he could have murdered anyone. At least, not out of anything but self-defense. But if it were self-defense, then he would not be wanted.

She bit her lip. Maybe it was all a mistake. Maybe someone had put up the poster because they were jealous of him. She glanced over her shoulder.

Trey was hard at work preparing the camp. His wide shoulders strained as he arranged the saddles. His sleeves were rolled up to his elbows. His forearms were strong and sleek. It reminded her that all of him was strong and sleek. Her body had lain against him. She knew every curve and plane.

She swallowed her desire and went back to picking up wood. Ethan needed her. The only way to help her brother was to betray Trey. The only way to save the boys was to turn in the man who had stolen her heart.

She didn't have any other choice.

"You've got a good load," he said behind her, startling her out of her thoughts. "Here. Let me take that."

He moved in close. The scent of wood and man invaded her senses. It was attraction plain and simple. An attraction so strong it left her breathless. Her heart sped up in her chest as he pulled the wood from her arms. His deep gaze no longer cut like ice, but instead melted her knees.

She swallowed hard. "It's not enough."

"It'll do for a start," he countered. "Why don't you go sit down and take off your jacket. I need to see what all this riding has done to your wound."

"It's fine," she lied. He was so breathtakingly handsome in the half-light. She fought the urge to reach out and touch the hard planes of his face.

"I bet it is," he said gruffly. "But I still need to look at it."

"We'll be in Durango in a couple of days. I'll see the doctor then."

"It could be so badly infected by then that you won't know me from the doctor," he said and turned toward the camp. "Go sit down before you fall down."

He walked away. His long lean legs strode firmly, making her weak in the knees. She had it bad. It was awful. It was worse than awful; it was catastrophic.

"He's no knight in shining armor," she muttered to herself. "He's a criminal." She picked her way through the stand of trees. He was right in one thing. If she didn't sit down soon, she was going to fall down.

Darn it. She had to be strong. She had Ethan to think about. She went over to the fire and sat. It felt so good she sighed with the pleasure of it.

"Take off your jacket and blouse," Trey ordered.

She opened her eyes to see him spitting a skinned rabbit. Since he had become free they had had fresh meat every night. It wasn't as if she could have done that, she reasoned. His brothers had been so close behind they didn't have the luxury of a fire.

His brothers!

"Where are they?"

He glanced up at her. "Who?"

"The gang that was chasing us, your brothers. Where are they?"

He went back to roasting the meat. "I guess you lost them," he said.

"I doubt that." She remembered that if her captive seemed comfortable then the posse must be near. Fear made her look around. She hadn't felt like they were being followed.

"Relax," he ordered. "There isn't anyone around for twenty miles."

"They found us, didn't they?" He didn't answer. "When? When did they catch up?"

"The day after the cat got you."

"But you didn't go back with them. Why?"

"You asked me not to leave you."

"I don't understand. Where did they go?"

"Home."

She chewed on that a while. "I see."

"What do you see?"

"They took one look at me and figured you weren't in any danger. So they went home."

He gathered up the stuff and began to make pan biscuits. "You were in pretty bad shape."

It frightened her to think of a gang of killers studying her while she slept. "Are your brothers wanted too?"

"I doubt it," he said. "Matt's the sheriff of Amesville. Tag, he ain't nothing but a horseman. If you're thinking about going after them for bounty you'll be disappointed. I don't remember ever seeing a poster for their arrest."

The strange fear lessened. She had not been in any danger. "So, tell me again what you did to get your name on a wanted poster?"

He put the biscuits on the flame to bake. "Only if you take off your coat and let me look at that wound."

She did as he commanded. It was strange, but she didn't feel shy around him anymore. They had spent too much time together.

He stepped across the fire and hunkered down beside her. He inspected her bandage, then untied the knotting holding it in place.

"So—"

"What?" he asked.

"So, tell me how you became a wanted man," she said. "It must be one heck of a story."

"Probably not as good a story as how you became a bounty hunter."

"How many men did you kill?" she countered. She wasn't sure she wanted him to know any more about her than he did. He was already far too intimate with her person. It would be worse if she confided in him. Trust was a foreign word. If she told him the truth, she would be at his mercy.

It was that kind of trust that had gotten Ethan in the predicament he was in. She had trusted her friend to watch over him, to take him in and treat him like a son. Instead the friend had put him on the orphan train and sent him off to the first couple who would take him.

In Ethan's case it had been those miners looking for slave labor.

"I haven't killed anyone," Trey said.

She looked into his eyes and could see the truth in his words. "I was afraid of that," she said.

He began to unwind the bandages over her wounds. "Disappointed, I see."

She went to shrug, but the movement made her wounds burn. "If you didn't kill anyone, then how did you get on a wanted poster?

"I told you. I left home a few years back."

"Yes, you said that."

"Well, my brothers had been looking for me to tell me that my parents were dead and that I had inherited the ranch."

"Didn't you write your own family?"

"I was . . . angry. When I'm angry, I'm not much of a human being."

"What made you so angry?"

"It's a long story."

"I've got nowhere to go."

"Fine. Katherine, my fiancée, was pregnant with my child when she decided I wasn't rich enough for her to marry. A wealthier man came into town, and she conveniently miscarried."

"No!"

"The midwife told me that Katherine had been in to see her."

"She couldn't save the baby?"

"She didn't want to. Katherine left two days later. I hear she's living in a mansion in San Francisco now.

"No wonder you were angry. You must feel like your child was taken from you."

"There was nothing I could do about it." He tossed the old bandage in the fire and looked back at her. "I swore I would have nothing to do with family ever again."

"I see." It seemed the best thing to say under the circumstances. It was clear he would never have anything to do with her. She came with a ready-made family. She swallowed the hurt that thought caused.

He bent down to examine her wound. He was so close to her that she could feel his breath on the bare skin of her shoulder. It made goosebumps up and down her arms.

His hands were so gentle. If she hadn't seen him tug the final bit of bandage off she would never have known that the wound was still oozing.

"Does that hurt?" he asked. He lifted his gaze. His face was a breath away from hers and she inhaled sharply. Another new emotion coursed through her. It warmed her and made her feel as if her limbs were made of jelly.

"What?" The word came out a whisper. It was as if all thought had fallen out of her head. The only thing in her world was Trey. He smelled so good. She wanted to taste him, even if it was just this once.

He must have read her mind because he leaned in and kissed her. She closed her eyes and savored the feel of his lips on hers, the smell of his skin, the warm pressure of his kiss—then nothing.

She opened her eyes to see that he had shifted away. His back was to her as he tore new bandages from her old petticoat. He had told her that the initial bandages came from his shirt, but he had soon run out of material. She had given up the petticoat. When he turned back, he did not look at her face. Instead he studied her wounds.

"You've irritated it with all the hard riding."

"I have to get to town."

"I'm going to have to clean it then. I'll get the whiskey."

"Is it going to hurt that bad?"

"I clean it with the whiskey."

"Oh."

"It's an old field trick."

"Yes, I read about that in Mr. Fry's book."

"Who?"

"Albert Fry's *Guide to the Wilderness*."

"Where the heck did you see such a thing and who would read it?"

"I saw it at the library, and I read it."

"I see." He said this with the most disbelieving tone.

"It was very informative."

He made what sounded like a snorting sound and pulled the whiskey bottle out of the pack.

"Why did you make that noise?"

"What noise?"

"That snorting noise."

He tore off a fold of her once useful petticoat and wadded it up. Then he poured whiskey on it and turned to her. "Anyone who really knows anything about the wilderness would not write a book about it."

"I see."

"This might sting a bit." He dabbed the whiskey-laden cloth on her wound. The sharp pain nearly took her breath away. "You okay?"

"Sure," she squeaked as her eyes teared. But the cruel man had no mercy. He cleaned another inch, and she thought if she could breathe she would scream, but right now both were out of the question.

He glanced up at her. "I could douse it all at once if you'd rather."

That idea did not thrill her. "What ever happened to soap and water?" Her question was a whisper, as she could not catch a breath.

"All we have for soap is lye, and I'm betting this whiskey is less painful than that would be." She winced at the thought. He reached over and handed her the bottle. "Here. Take a few swigs."

This time she did not hesitate. The heat of the liquor going down her throat distracted her enough for him to dab farther down her shoulder. She gulped, and he worked on her arm.

The world spun around her and her head was light. She wasn't sure if it was from the whiskey or her inability to breathe. It didn't matter.

She tried to wrap her thoughts around to the original conversation. The one where he was telling her how he ended up on a wanted poster. "So," she said. The word sounded oddly slurred. He snatched the whiskey bottle out of her hand.

"So?"

"So, you didn't write home and your brothers put a thousand–dollar reward on your head." She frowned. "That doesn't make any sense at all."

"Honey, in your current condition I could tell you the sky was blue and it wouldn't make any sense," he said as he worked.

She looked down and was surprised to see that he was two thirds of the way done. Her flesh was raised up and bright red, but there was no oozing and no ugly color. "The stitches don't look bad. I guess your Ma was a good teacher."

"Well now, on that I have to agree."

She reached out and brushed the hair away from his forehead and he froze. "I bet she would be crying her eyes out if she found out you were a wanted man."

"I'm not wanted."

"I want you." The words came out of nowhere. She blinked when she realized she was the one who said them.

"That's the whiskey talkin'."

"Okay," she agreed. He went back to cleaning her wound. After a few last dabs, he tore a new bandage off the petticoat and wound it around her arm.

The movement caught her attention. She concentrated on the gentle heat and pressure from his fingers. They moved in an amazingly sensual way. Again it sent the shivers up her skin.

"You cold?"

"Yeah," she answered.

"I'll be done in a minute," he said. "Then I'll see to the fire."

He finished his task in silence and as soon as her bandage was secure, he draped her jacket over her shoulders. She huddled inside it and watched him build the fire.

When the pain in her arm had subsided she realized she was tired, bone–numbing tired. He moved with easy grace and, while the rabbit cooked, created another rich meal out of the beans, cornmeal, and flour she had brought as supplies.

She laid her head down on her saddle. "Did your ma teach you how to cook too?"

"Nope."

"Then how did you learn?"

"My pa taught us. When we were old enough to help with the spring roundup, Pa insisted we learn how to cook." He paused, then asked. "How did you learn how to shoot?"

"My pa taught me when I was young. He said a girl should be able to defend herself."

"Smart man."

"Yes, as I told you before, he was a professor of letters. He taught me how to read."

"That why you spend so much time in the library?"

"Yep," she yawned and closed her eyes. "That, and the fact that I'm a librarian."

"You're a librarian?"

"Uh huh." The heat from the fire warmed her faced. It felt so good to lie under the stars and smell the dampening earth, to hear the fire pop and listen to the sounds of Trey making biscuits. She realized that these small things had become her world.

How very strange and different it was from the world she left. The world of books and beeswax and the scraping sounds of chairs being pulled out and pushed back in.

"Unbelievable."

"What?"

"Where's your daddy now?"

"I told you, he and Ma died when I was nine."

"What happened?"

"Train wreck."

"I'm sorry."

"It was a long time ago."

"Well, get some rest, dinner will be ready soon."

"Okay." He hadn't pressed for more information. It was at that moment she realized it didn't matter how he had gotten himself on a wanted poster. He was a nice man and probably innocent. That meant one thing. She couldn't turn him in.

* * *

He kissed her. He couldn't help it. She looked so beautiful lying beside the fire, her hair flowing about her. He remembered the shocking heat of the first time he had kissed her. Heat lightning had struck the base of his spine and he'd wanted to grab her, hold her in his arms and kiss her good.

The desire had been so strong that he had pulled back before he had gotten a proper taste. It was the only thing he could do. She was too much a lady. Bounty hunter or not, her kiss proved she was as innocent as a newborn calf.

She smelled of sweet earth, crushed flowers, and whiskey. It made him smile. She had swallowed enough to put a strong man halfway under the table. But he understood that the pain in her shoulder had to be great, though she never complained.

He couldn't imagine it. The only female he had ever known to be so strong had been his ma. She was nothing like his ma. She was more like the sleeping beauty in the fairy tale his ma had told him when he was young.

For a moment he indulged himself in the fantasy and kissed her full on those sweet red lips. They were soft and warm and she smiled just before she kissed him back.

That smile ripped his heart out of his chest and branded him hers.

Chapter Ten

Regretfully, Brianna eased her way out of the bedding. Trey reached for her but did not open his eyes.

"I have to go do the necessary," she whispered.

He grunted and let her go. She crept to a full stand. Her head pounded with the aftereffects of whiskey; her shoulder pulled and ached. But she knew there was only one thing to do.

She had to leave.

If she stayed, Trey would follow her into town. Heck, he'd take her into town, and who knew what would happen then. His face was plastered all over the place, with a thousand-dollar reward listed underneath it in big bold letters. The first crazy old miner to recognize him might just get lucky and kill him. She couldn't have the murder of an innocent man on her soul.

She managed to get her horse saddled without waking Trey. She knew he was a light sleeper. It would be only the sheerest luck if she could get away.

She glanced over at her saddlebags. They were packed for tomorrow's ride, but they rested near his head. She just couldn't risk it.

She took what she had. The clothes on her back, her horse and saddle and the rifle. Brianna glanced over at Trey's sleeping form. Her heartbeat sped up filled with tenderness and affection. The man was a dream. Some woman, somewhere, would wear him down and marry him, maybe even convince him to have a family with her. She just knew it. She reached up and touched her lips. He had kissed her. She could tell. Her mouth felt soft and alive.

Alive. That's how she wanted to keep him, and to do that she had to leave him. She climbed into the saddle and barely contained a moan. It would be rough riding at first. There was a moon, but the ground was still new to her. Then she'd have to double back and sidetrack a few times until she lost him.

She sighed. She had to lose him. It could mean his very life. She nudged her horse forward and eased into the wilderness. If he were to wake in the next few minutes it would all be over, but if he slept, even for fifteen minutes, he would be safe.

She said a prayer that he would sleep, and eased into the darkness without looking back.

Trey woke up in a rush, all his senses on alert at the possibility of danger. Something wasn't right. His gun was in his hand before he stood. He glanced around the camp. Nothing moved.

Then he saw it. One of the horses was missing and Bri was gone. He cursed under his breath. Somehow she had slipped away into the night. He glanced at the lightening sky. She couldn't have gotten too far away.

He pulled on his jacket, cleaned up the camp, and saddled his horse in a hurry. He scowled. She had left him all the supplies except the shotgun. She had had sense enough to take it.

He shook his head. How could she have gotten past him? He was sleeping right beside her. It wasn't like him at all to let something so important slip away.

He must be getting old.

Trey hitched himself up into the saddle and calmed his anger with a deep breath. He knew her tracks would be hard to follow, but he hadn't been with her this long for nothing. He knew the method to her back-tracking. He was certain it wouldn't take long to find her.

Then he would find out why she felt she had to run away from him.

Brianna arrived in Durango, trail-hardened and scarred.

She stopped at the livery and stabled her horse. Then she took her shotgun with her and got a room at the hotel. She paid extra to have a bath drawn in the small room down the hall. She wanted to be clean even more than she wanted to eat—and she was pow-erfully hungry.

The bath water was hot and smooth. It was the best thing Bri had felt on her skin since she'd slept with Trey. A sudden picture of his warm, well-built body popped into her mind. Sadness welled up inside her. She had gone and done it. She had fallen in love.

What a stupid, hopeless thing to do.

She took a deep breath, then slid under the surface of the water and listened to her heartbeat thudding against her chest. The water lapped above her and her stomach growled.

She released her breath and resurfaced. She didn't have time to feel sorry for herself. She only had two days to come up with a new plan to save Ethan and, if she could, to save the other boys.

Time was awasting.

She scrubbed the trail dust off with a vengeance and enjoyed the small sliver of violet-smelling soap that the hotel had provided.

She didn't have much money left. She figured that she would need at least one new outfit. Those miners had to think she had money or they would spit in her face.

She calculated quickly. A new outfit, bait money, and a way out of town fast. It was going to be very tight.

Bri knew it was a day and a half straight shot to Trademark, Nevada. That was the closest train station. If she could somehow get her brother away from the miners, then they would need two train tickets back to Boston. If she managed to save all the boys, they'd have to ride back home too.

It was an impossible task.

She refused to worry about it. Instead she scrubbed her hair and rinsed it, then set about washing her trail clothes. She would need them in two days. If they had to, they could cross the country on horseback.

She had gone from Wyoming to Nevada once. She could do it again.

Trey was madder than a hornet with a disturbed nest. The bounty hunter had managed to elude him for three days. She had to be in town. So he had given up and come straight in. He swore he would hunt her down and when he did, it was going to be a show-down.

She owed him. What, he wasn't exactly sure of, but she owed him something for dragging him all this way from his ranch. First off, he was going to see the sheriff and have those wanted posters pulled down. Then he was going to get a bath and a good meal.

Then he was going hunting. It wouldn't be too hard. There was only one hotel in town and two boarding houses. The way he figured it, she was staying at one.

He tied his horse up in front of the jail and strode in. It was odd not having his boots, but he figured Jeb would understand.

"Well, look what the cat dragged in," Will Mackenzie hollered. Will was deputy of Durango and had gotten to know Trey real well during the week he'd been detained and waited for his brother to arrive. "You come back to lose at poker?"

Disgusted, Trey reached up and tugged the wanted

poster off the wall. "Will, how many of these things do you still have up?"

"Just a couple," Will said. He grinned. "It shouldn't matter seein' as though everyone knows the bounty's been paid."

"Take them down, now."

Will stood. "What's got your tail in a bunch?"

"These posters got me kidnapped and hauled half-way here."

"How can that be? We sent out the notice that the bounty was paid."

"Well, not everyone got the message. Someone saw this poster and almost brought my carcass back for the reward."

Will laughed out loud. "Ha, that's a good one. Ain't nobody slick enough to bring you back here dead or alive."

"Oh, this one was slick enough," Trey said. He lifted his foot. "Took my boots and my weapons."

"Now, that ain't right, taking a man's boots."

The door to the jail burst open and Jeb Walker strode in. He was a huge man, bigger even than Trey or his brothers, and his voice boomed like a cannon. "Well, heck fire, it's Trey Morgan. What brings you back to these parts?"

Trey had just enough time to brace himself before Jeb reached over and grabbed Trey in a bear hug. Trey winced as his arms were squeezed against his chest. Trey held on as the steel bands tightened and pushed all the air out of his lungs. His feet were hauled off the floor and then he was slammed back down.

"Good to see ya!" Jeb said and slapped him on the back. Then he picked at the opening of Trey's jacket. "Where the heck is your shirt? Didn't your ma teach you how to dress?"

"Check out his feet," Will said with a smirk.

"Now Trey, only crazy men walk around without boots. Did those used to be socks on your feet?"

Trey rubbed his arms to get some blood back into them and glanced down at his bare toes hanging out of his once–good socks. "That's why I'm here."

"Trey says some bounty hunter saw the wanted posters and tried to drag him in. Seems he took his boots so he wouldn't run away. Probably took his shirt too."

"Now that's nearly a killin' offense. Did you set him straight?"

"I'm here, aren't I? Now, take down these darned posters." Trey waved the paper he held in his hand under Jeb's nose. "I've got to go get some new boots and stable my horse."

That caught Jeb's attention. "You figure on sticking around here for a while?"

"A couple of days."

"Who you hunting?" Jeb asked. He crossed his arms over his chest.

"That's between me and them."

"You let us know if you need any help."

"Yeah." Will piped up, then spit between the floor planks. "Let us know. I'll have the jail all cleaned out and ready."

Trey opened the door. "You do that. See you later."

"Trey?" Jeb called.

"Yeah?"

"When you're settled, there's a good bottle of whiskey and a fresh pack of playing cards waiting for you."

What she needed was a plan. Brianna never did anything important without a clear plan. Her trail clothes were sturdy and nondescript enough to allow her to blend in with the locals. She spent the morning walking the sidewalks of town and studying it from every angle.

From the back of the saloon, she and Ethan could slip through two alleys and go into the back of the church. She figured it was the last place the miners would think to look. Especially since she planned to double back around the shed that led to the stable.

But she wouldn't be going to the stable. She would have horses saddled and gear stored and ready behind the school's outhouse. It was a two-seater and wide enough to conceal the horses, at least some of them.

Tomorrow was Sunday, her day of reckoning. If her plan worked they would be out of Durango as soon as it turned dark. She'd already been to the land office and memorized the maps that would take them back through the mountains.

It was a good solid plan as long as she could get the boys out of the saloon. A sense of doom came over her. She needed more money. There was no way she could steal horses, and they might need as many as fifteen if the miners had given her a correct count of the boys.

Somehow, some way, she'd have to come up with the money for the horses by tomorrow afternoon.

"You planning on robbing the bank?"

Brianna stopped in her tracks. That sounded like Trey's voice. She shook her head. It couldn't be. There was no reason for him to come to Durango and every reason for him to go home.

She took another step.

"Yep, robbing the bank, that's what I think you're planning."

She turned. Her heart rate sped up. There, sitting on a chair outside the barber shop, was Trey—right out in the open, where anyone could see him and shoot him.

"What do you think you're doing?" she asked and moved in front of him. She wasn't big enough to hide him from view, but maybe she could block it a little. "You could get killed."

He looked her up and down. "You thinkin' about killing me?"

"No, but that doesn't mean you're safe." She grabbed his arm and tugged him off the chair and around the corner.

He grinned at her. "Why, Miss Bri, I didn't think you cared."

"I cared enough to leave you three days away from here. You were safe. Why did you come here?"

His deep, ice–blue eyes glittered. "You didn't say goodbye."

She was more frightened for him than she was for her brother Ethan. Confound it! She had it bad. "You don't seem to understand. There are wanted posters up all over town with your face on them."

"You mean this?" He held out a poster.

She yanked it out of his hand and crumpled it up. "Why are you acting like an idiot? A thousand dollars is a lot of money. Some loon is going to shoot you in the back, no questions asked."

"Honey, it's so nice to hear you worry over me."

Frustrated, she stomped her foot. "Will you just leave? Look, I know a back way to the stables from here. If you need my help, I can—"

He grabbed her and kissed her. Hard. Every thought fled from her head. He was here. Big and hard and smelled so good, she thought she would surely die. The kiss was not gentle at first, but she wrapped her hands around his neck and hung on with the storm.

He gentled the kiss, then broke off to press his lips to her temple, her cheek, her hair. "You scared me." His words were hoarse and full of unspoken emotion. "I kept picturing you hurt somewhere and I wouldn't be able to get to you."

She hugged him close. He smelled so right, like fresh mountain air and man and a hint of good soap. Somewhere along the line she had fallen in love and no denying it.

"I couldn't bring you back to town." She leaned back to look up into his face. "Seriously, someone would kill you. And I couldn't say goodbye."

"Why?"

She didn't want to tell him the truth—didn't want to make it real. It would take too much. It would take trust; and she wasn't ready for that yet. She doubted she ever would be ready.

"I'm pretty certain you wouldn't let me say good-bye."

"Darn right. Now where are you staying?"

"I'm staying at the hotel."

"What a coincidence. So am I."

"You can't stay with me."

He shot her an interesting look. "I didn't plan on it."

She blew out a breath of relief. At least, she told herself it was relief. Her heart pounded with attraction and sadness. "You can't stay in this town," she said again. "You're going to get killed."

He grabbed her hand and pulled her deeper into the shadows. "I think I deserve an explanation."

"What kind of explanation? I told you why I left. I'm pretty certain it was a good reason."

He drew a deep breath, sighed loudly, and contemplated her. "Let's start from the beginning. Why did you arrest me?"

"I needed the money."

"Then why didn't you bring me in?"

"You said you were innocent and I believed you."

"Just like that, you believed me?"

"You didn't act like a murderer."

"Really. How would a murderer act?"

"To begin with, a murderer would have left me at the first opportunity," she said. "You stayed and tended to me. You didn't take anything from me, and you didn't seem worried at all that I was headed back to Durango. I admit it was a crazy story you told, but I thought it had to be true. A murderer would not risk his life for me."

"Even if he fell in love with you?"

Her heart leaped with joy and fear. A rushing sound started in her ears and she wasn't sure she heard him right. "Excuse me?"

He towered over her until she was backed up against the side of the building. "I said a murderer would risk his life for you if he had fallen in love with you."

She clutched the wooded shingle behind her. It felt rough against her fingertips, but it was solid and real. The rest of the world had gone spinning out of control.

"Why would he do that?"

"I don't know," he said and leaned into her. "It could be your beauty. That fine skin of yours, the silk of your hair." He was a breath away. "The rose of your lips."

She swallowed. "A man would risk his life for that?"

He kissed her then. A short sweet kiss. "I would risk my life for your kiss."

Her knees gave way from under her. He grabbed her and pulled her into his arms. "So," she said as his mouth descended toward hers. "Do you know your life is at risk?"

He halted a hair's breadth away. A scowl formed on his face and he lifted his head back. "Do you want to turn me in?"

Stunned, she pushed him away. "No. How could you think that of me?"

"You said you needed the money. I happen to know you didn't get any on the trail here."

Confusion, anger, and disappointment filled her, washing away the joy she had felt in his arms. "I can't believe you still think I would turn you in for the bounty." She turned her back on him and stormed down the alley. Tears stung the back of her eyes. This was stupid. She had been stupid to think he would trust her, might actually love her. That she might actually love him.

She was a fool.

"Wait."

"I think we're through," she said and turned toward the church.

He grabbed her arm and spun her to face him. "I think we're a long way from through."

"Why. Because you still want to kiss me? Maybe you want to spend the night in my bed?"

He glanced around, then frowned at her. "Keep it down."

"What's the matter? Are you afraid you might get shot?"

"I don't give a damn about getting shot."

"Well, you should," she said and shook her head. "You were a fool to follow me here and I was fool enough to care."

"You said you believed that I was innocent."

"I do."

"Then why did you ask me if I expected you to turn me in?"

"I don't know," she said. "I don't know why I'm even talking to you."

"Look, I'm sorry. This isn't going right."

"Oh, and how's it supposed to go? What is it you want from me, Trey Morgan? I already set you free. I let you go so you could go home and be safe. Heck, I even shielded you from sight for fear you might get killed. I don't have time for this."

She turned and hurried down the alley. He followed behind her. She ignored him the best she could and stepped into the cool quiet of the church.

Her emotions were all over the place. She didn't know whether to laugh or cry or just be really, really angry. She moved down the aisle and into a pew.

The church was abandoned except for her and Trey, who moved in beside her. It was cool in the dusky afternoon and smelled of prayer books and polished wood.

The pews were smooth to the touch and hard against her back.

"I don't know why you need the money, but I think I can help," Trey said.

Brianna did not want to hear any more from him. She clasped her hands and closed her eyes. Maybe, if she pretended to pray, he would take the hint and leave her alone.

He didn't.

"Dear Lord," he began. "I want you to know I forgive Brianna for dragging me back to Durango."

She opened her eyes. He looked as innocent as you please with his eyes closed and his hands folded. "I did not drag you here."

"Please help her to see the light and give her the strength not to rob the bank."

"I am not going to rob the bank."

He opened his eyes. "It sure looked to me like you were planning a bank heist."

She blew out her breath in exasperation. "I tell you, I'm not going to rob the bank!"

"Then tell me what you are going to do."

"Why?"

"Maybe I can help you."

"Why would you do that?"

"I don't have a clue," he said. "I just feel the need. So are you going to tell me?"

"No. What I am going to do is go to the saloon." She got up. He followed.

"What are you going to do there?"

"I need money."

He grabbed her arm. "You are not the kind of girl to do that for money."

"I can so do that," she said indignant. "I have read all the books on the subject. I know perfectly well how to do it."

"See here, it's not morally right for a woman like you to do that."

"What, I suppose you think you can do it better than me?"

That made him pause and take a step back. She left

the church. The shadows were growing longer and soon the sun would set.

"What are you talking about?"

"Why, playing poker, of course," she said. "I suppose you think you can play better than me."

A look of relief washed over him. She thought she heard him mutter something like "thank goodness." That stopped her in her tracks. "What did you think I was going to do in that saloon?"

"Never mind," he said and took a hold of her arm. "Have you had dinner yet?"

"No, but I don't have time for that. I have to win some money."

"Then you're in luck. I happen to have scheduled a poker game for after dinner. Come on. I'll treat you to dinner, and then you can come and watch me play a few hands. If you think you're better than I am, then you can go on to the saloon. If not, I'll win your money for you."

"How much can you win?"

"How much do you need?"

"There's not enough money in this town for what I need," she said. "But I can make two hundred work."

"No problem."

She bit her bottom lip. "All right, but I can't take your winnings from you unless you play with my money."

"Sounds fair. How much do you have?"

"How much will I need?"

"Do you have a twenty?"

She smiled in relief. "Yes, I do."

"Then let's go get some dinner."

"Wait! It's not safe."

He put her hand in the crook of his arm and escorted her toward the only restaurant in town. "Now, sweetheart, trust me, I can take care of myself."

"All right," she said reluctantly, "if you say so."

"I say so."

"So, where is this poker game?"

"At the jailhouse."

She blinked. Her fear of the sheriff finding out about her plans grew. She bit her lip.

"I *told* you the bounty was paid. The sheriff and I are friends." He glanced at her sideways. "Aren't you glad you didn't bring my dead carcass in?"

Chapter Eleven

"Does it have to be the jailhouse?" she asked.

"Trust me, Jeb's going to be kind. He's a big guy, but he's all heart."

"Sure he is," she said. Her fear rose sharply. "Unless you're a criminal, right?"

"Of course," Trey said, "but no worries. I told you I was innocent."

She frowned at the night air. She knew *she* wasn't innocent. If the sheriff got word of what she was about to do, she'd be in all kinds of trouble. She'd be lucky to get out of town without a bounty on her own head.

Zeke's words came back to her. "An' don't think you can go to the sheriff neither, missy," Zeke had said. "He'll as likely arrest you as us. It's against the law to try to buy these here boys. I'll be sure to tell him you made the first offer an' I have a whole saloon full of witnesses. Old Jeb will haul you away in hand-cuffs."

It was going to be a long and terrible night. She needed the money, so she had to play. She would just have to watch every word out of her mouth, or the sheriff might become suspicious.

"So tell me how you came to know Trey?" Jeb asked as he dealt out the first round of cards.

Trey winced. He hoped she wouldn't tell the sheriff and his deputy that she had arrested Trey. He wasn't looking forward to another round of humiliation.

Bri didn't even look at him. Instead, she smiled warmly. "He saved my life."

Now that was not what he expected her to say. Intrigued, he leaned back in his chair and pretended to watch the smooth, well-worn cards in his hand.

"Is that so?"

"Yes, you see, I was attacked by a huge mountain lion. Lucky for me, Trey just happened to be bathing in a nearby stream."

Jeb raised an eyebrow, but Trey ignored him. "I suppose he leaped out of the water as naked as a baby and kilt the thing with his bare hands."

"Well, he didn't exactly use his bare hands. But he managed to slit the cat's throat."

"Sounds like a regular hero to me," Will said with a smirk.

"Trey, how the heck, pardon my expression, ma'am, did you manage to do that?" Jed asked.

Trey contemplated his cards, while a sense of admiration and pride washed over him. "She had already emptied her handgun in the cat's gut."

Jeb turned back to Bri. "So the little lady can shoot."

"Better than most men I know," Trey said and tossed out the first bet.

"Now that's saying something," Jeb said and added his money to the kitty. "I guess I have to apologize then."

"Why?"

"I had you figured for a greenhorn."

"I beg your pardon."

"Someone who spent their whole life in the city back east," he explained. "I don't figure they have much call to be teaching their fine ladyfolk how to shoot."

She laughed. The sound did something warm and pleasant to Trey's gut. "I'm terribly sorry, I'm not laughing at you. You see, you're right. I'm from Boston. I was born and raised there."

"So, what's a lady like you do?" Will asked as he tossed in his coin. "I mean, that you would learn how to shoot so good."

"I'm afraid you'll be terribly disappointed."

"Tell us, you have my curiosity up," Jeb said.

"She's a librarian," Trey said.

"A librarian?"

"I work for the Boston Public Library," Bri answered.

"Didn't know they had cause for shootin' in the library," Will said.

"No, I didn't learn to shoot in the library," she said. "My pa taught me the basics and I read up on the subject. Did you know there are a multitude of techniques out there? I find the English side-arm technique works best for me."

By now all the men were leaning back in their chairs and staring at her.

"Are you telling us that you learned to shoot by reading a book on the subject?" Jeb's tone of voice was incredulous. Trey felt the same way.

"Well, I did go out to the range and practice a few times. Pa said I had a natural talent for it."

"Did you hear that? She's got a natural talent for it."

"What else did you learn in that library of yours?" Jeb asked.

"I learned about tracking and wilderness survival."

"Did they leave out the part about mountain lions?" Trey asked.

She looked at him. "No. I believe I was distracted at the time of the attack."

Trey remembered sharply the moment when he'd stripped his clothes off and entered the water. He glanced at the men around the table and realized that they also had an idea of what had distracted her.

"I'll call." He said drawing their attention back to the game. "Full house."

The men threw in their cards and he collected the money. Brianna was a puzzle. He wasn't sure she was telling the truth, but the story was so fantastic it had to be true. It was as offbeat and unbelievable as her kidnapping him and dragging him halfway through the wilderness while keeping his brothers at bay.

"So, what else did you learn in the library, Brianna?" Will asked.

"Well," she said. "I learned how to play poker."

"Really?" Jeb grinned. "There's a lot more to the game than what they put in those books."

"That's what Trey told me," she said. "So I came to watch."

"Hey, Jeb," Will said with a grin. "Let's let her play. Just one hand. I want to see what they told her in the book."

Curious, Trey watched Jeb mull it over. "Why not? This is a friendly game. You want to lose your money, darlin'?"

She pulled her chair in closer, mesmerizing him with the sweet scent of violets. "All I have is ten dollars. I was going to buy a new hat, but what the heck. I've always wanted to play a real game of poker."

Trey had the sneaking suspicion that they were all being had.

"Deal her in, Jeb," Will said. "Let's see what the little lady knows."

Brianna counted her money as Trey walked her back to the hotel. She had managed to win the two hundred she needed and keep the sheriff from suspecting she was up to anything extraordinary.

"Can I ask you a question?"

"Sure," she said glancing at Trey. His face was hidden in shadows. It was well into the night by the time the men gave up on beating her. Trey had bowed out two hours earlier.

"If you're so good at cards, why did you have to come all the way to Wyoming and drag me here?"

"I beg your pardon?"

"If you needed money, why didn't you just play poker for it?"

"Men don't like to let a woman play," she said as she stepped up onto the wooden sidewalk that flanked the hotel. "I tried to get into a few games, but no one was willing to play me. They said they couldn't take candy from babies or money from ladies."

He stopped her outside the glass front door of the hotel. "What do you need the money for?"

It was a direct question. One she didn't want to answer. "It doesn't matter now," she evaded. "It's too late to get the kind of money I needed."

He took a hold of her arm. "Look, heaven knows I'm a patient man. I've never crossed you. Why can't you trust me?"

She swallowed. Fear rose up inside her. After her parents' death, it had taken years for her to trust. Then the one person she trusted with her brother's life betrayed her. She didn't have to learn that lesson twice. "I trust you," she lied.

"Then tell me what drove you clear out to Wyoming."

"I told you it no longer matters."

"Then what do you need the two hundred dollars for? Are you in trouble?"

She stepped back. "Good night, Trey. Thank you for the dinner and the game."

"If you really trust me, you'll tell me. Tell me, Bri."

Darkness swelled around them, closing in until they were the only two people on the face of the earth. She looked into his handsome face and something deep in her heart began to crack open. Love meant trust. She couldn't truly say she loved him until she trusted him with her secrets.

Her heart pounded at the risk she took. If he betrayed her, it would be the worst hurt of her whole life. She studied his face. She had to trust him.

"I have a younger brother," she said. The words came out slow and painful. She swallowed and licked her lips. "His name is Ethan. When my parents died we were both sent to the orphanage. I tried to protect him; but the orphanage was sold off and closed down, and the girls went to Miss Bush's Home for Young Ladies. The boys were sent to New York City, to the West Side Lodging Home for Homeless Boys." Her voice cracked with the distress she felt.

"Go on."

"I wrote Ethan every day. I promised that as soon as I turned sixteen, I was going to get a job and get him out of there." She looked into his face and saw compassion. "It was not a good place," she whispered.

"What happened?"

"I got a job at the Boston Public Library. It paid just enough to support me, but I pinched pennies until I had enough to send for Ethan." She stopped and took a deep breath. "It took me three years, but I did it. I sent the money to a friend from the orphanage days who lived in New York. She was to go get Ethan, buy two train tickets to Boston and escort him to me."

"Somehow I get the feeling that isn't what happened."

"No." Bri bit the inside of her cheek to keep her emotions in check. She didn't want Trey to see the shame she felt.

"What happened?"

"I waited three months," Bri whispered. "She had said it would take time to make all the arrangements. When I didn't hear from her, I wired her, but she never answered. So, I wired the orphanage." She stopped and took a deep breath. "It was then that I discovered what had happened."

"She took the money."

"Yes. She took the money. She never even stopped at the orphanage. There was an outbreak of scarlet fever in the city and the orphanages became overloaded. So they started sending the boys out on orphan trains."

"Orphan trains?"

"They packed children on trains and sent them west. The hope was that they would find good homes on farms and ranches. Places with clean air and wide open spaces."

"Your brother?"

"He was on one of those trains. No one told me. They just sent him off. So, I took a leave of absence from my job and I followed the train. I stopped wherever it stopped and I searched every town."

"Did you find him?"

"Yes, I found him. He was sent here. Two miners took him. They claim to have adopted him, but they were using him for slave labor. I told them I was taking him, but they said I had to pay them to get him back."

"Let me guess. They want some outrageous amount."

"I didn't know what to do, until I spied your wanted poster. The bounty would have been enough to pay for my brother."

"Then what?"

She shrugged. "I don't know. I guess I'd take him back to Boston and see if I couldn't get my job back."

"Bri, what they are doing is wrong. It's akin to slavery. You should have gone to the sheriff."

She shuddered and hugged herself. "I didn't know the sheriff. I didn't trust the sheriff."

"Why?"

She glanced at him. "In the orphanage you learned early not to trust anyone in authority. Not to trust anyone but yourself." She studied the sky. "I only broke that rule once."

"When you sent your friend the money."

"Yes—and I told you how that worked out."

"So, you set off to bring me in."

"So, I set off to bring you to justice and rescue my brother."

"But you didn't."

"I didn't."

"Now what?"

She shrugged. "I have a different plan."

He gently put his hands on her shoulders and turned her toward him. "What is your plan, Bri?"

"I'm going to have to try and negotiate for less money."

"Bri, darling, that isn't going to work."

"It has to work," she said. "Ethan looked so pale. They beat him, Trey." She sobbed. "They beat him and the other boys."

His grip on her shoulders tightened. "What other boys?"

"The other boys off the orphan train. They told me that there were fifteen all together." She begged him to understand. "I couldn't stand to see it. I thought nothing was worse than the orphanage. But this, Trey, this is worse."

"Fifteen boys?"

"I know, it's a lot, but I'm not leaving one behind." She took a deep breath. "So now you know. You know exactly what is going on."

He was silent so long she thought her heart would break, but she kept her mouth closed. She was not going to make a decision for him.

"Come on," he said and took her hand.

"Where are we going?"

"To see my friend Jeb."

"We can't," she said and pulled her hand away from his. "The miners told me the sheriff would arrest me for attempting to buy the boys. Don't you see? If I'm in jail, then there isn't any way to help these boys."

He stopped and drew her against him. "I know you're afraid. But you have to trust me."

"Don't tell the sheriff, Trey. If you do—"

"Hush. Don't worry. Trust me, Bri."

"Promise me you won't tell the sheriff." He leaned down and kissed her. The kiss was comforting, yet fierce—as if he had made a decision. "Trust me."

She did, even though she was afraid to find out what would happen next.

Trey realized that Brianna would never talk to Jeb. So he sent her to her room. He told her to meet the miners just like she planned, but not to negotiate with them. He had a plan and she would have to trust him that it would work.

She reluctantly told him good night. He kissed her, and her knees went weak and her eyes fluttered closed. Then he gently pushed her into her room and closed the door.

He could only hope the kiss was enough to distract her. He went to his own room and waited half an hour before he headed off to see Jeb.

Fifteen boys. How could he go from a sworn bachelor to a husband and father of fifteen boys? It was nuts. His brothers would never believe it.

He felt like the happiest man on earth.

The only thing that stood between him and this new dream was Bri. He knew how hurt she was. Would she be able to trust him to help her? Would she understand that he had to go to Jeb?

He opened the jail door and strode in. "Put on a pot of coffee, Jeb. We have some talking to do."

She thought she had planned for every outcome, but she never expected this.

There were thirty miners in the saloon and fifteen half-starved boys ranging in age from eight to sixteen.

"You said you would pay a thousand dollars for the best boy," one miner said. He shoved a scrawny boy toward her. "This here's Jessie. He's all of twelve and can put in a solid day's work. Show her your muscle, son."

The little boy flexed his arm. "I washed up for ya too, miss. My ma used ta say I was handsome."

"That ain't nothing," another miner said and pushed himself and his boy to the front of the bar. "This here's Mick. He's sixteen and can work twenty-four hours straight if you whip him a little."

The young man named Mick was nearly her size, but he stared at his feet. His shoulders slumped.

Brianna's heart went out to him and to all the other boys, who looked to her for acceptance, delivery, and hope. Then there were a few that kept a hopeless, blank stare. She knew that look from the orphanage. They just didn't care any more.

She swallowed. Trey had told her to meet the miners as planned and wait for him. But he was late—and in the face of this crowd, serious doubts had begun to form in her mind.

The afternoon sun pounded on the tin roof, heating the air inside the saloon, which smelled of unwashed bodies and old liquor. The miners kept up a constant chorus of hacking coughs, probably gained from long hours in the deep, damp mines. No one seemed to notice. No one but her.

The crowd intimidated her more than she cared to admit.

But what she needed was to think on her feet. The first thing she needed to do was to find her brother and make sure he was all right. Then she needed to separate the boys from the men.

"Where's Ethan?" she asked.

"He's here, fat and happy just like you wanted," Zeke said, pulling Ethan up to the front. "Now this bargain was between you an' us. So, don't even be thinkin' you'll take some other boy. This here's the one ya came lookin' for."

Ethan glanced up at Bri. His eyes were alert and ready to help her in any way he could.

"Let me see him." She reached for Ethan.

"Let's see the money first," the miner said and yanked the boy behind him.

Bri was ready for this. Heart pounding with anticipation, she unlatched the satchel and held it open. She knew she would have to stall and wait for Trey, so she had stuffed the satchel with paper and laid the money she won last night on top.

The man peered inside. "Looks all there," he said and reached for the bag.

She snapped it shut. "I want to see the boy first," she said.

The crowd murmured and surged slightly forward.

The hair on the back of her neck rose. "My boy is better," someone in the back shouted. "I think you should look at him before ya make up yer mind."

There was a rumble of agreement.

"Fine, have the boys line up here." She pointed to the side of the bar. The boys fell into line, some eagerly, others reluctantly. "That's good," she said. Then she positioned herself between the boys and the miners. "Now let me look."

The boys' backs were to the saloon's back door. She had done it purposefully with the hope of making a clean getaway; but without Trey she had no idea how she was going to escape with fifteen boys.

She looked at the first in line. "What's your name?"

"Jeremy."

"How old are you, Jeremy?"

"Eight, ma'am."

"Do you work in the mine?"

"Yes, ma'am. I work twelve hours a day and don't complain much."

"I see. What's your name?" she asked the next in line.

"Adam."

"How old are you, Adam?"

"I'm thirteen, ma'am."

"Do you have any other skills?"

"Ma'am?"

"Can you do things other than mining?"

"Yes, ma'am, I can farm and I have a good hand with cattle."

She went down the entire line and took her time.

Each boy was as good as the next. She felt the crowd behind her growing restless and her own desperation growing too. *Where was Trey?*

"Hello, Ethan. Have they been treating you well?"

"Since I saw you last," he replied. "What have you got planned?" he whispered.

"Just follow my lead," she reassured him. "I'll get us out of here."

She moved back to the middle of the line and turned to face the crowd. "Well, gentlemen. You have given me a fine selection. So fine in fact it will be hard to choose."

"Just choose," someone hollered. "Or we'll choose for ya!"

The crowd murmured its agreement and began to surge forward. "We'll choose for ya!"

She grabbed the satchel and held it high. "Step back."

The crowd still came forward.

"You heard the lady, step back." It was Trey's deep commanding voice that had the crowd under control. He pushed through and stood behind the boys with his arms crossed. "Now why don't you tell me what exactly is going on here?"

Bri's heart and soul sang at the sight of him. It was going to be all right.

"I asked what is going on here," Trey said in the silence.

"I'll tell you," Melvin said as he pushed his way to Trey. The crowd began talking all at once. Trey pulled out his gun and let go a shot. The room was instantly silent.

"All right, tell me."

"This here, lady wants to buy my boy."

Trey swung his glance around to Brianna. She held her breath.

He turned back to Melvin. "Why are there so many boys here?"

"She said she wanted the ones off the orphan train," someone shouted from the back. "She offered two hundred dollars for Zeke's boy, but he said it wasn't enough. He said she had to pay him a thousand dollars."

Trey glared at Bri. "Slave trading is illegal."

She held out her hand and Ethan walked over to her. "This is my brother, Ethan," she said, her trust wavering. "This man wouldn't let me take him home unless I paid for him."

"She ain't paying me for the boy," Zeke said quickly when Trey turned his way. "She's paying me fer the loss of a worker an' my expenses in keepin' the boy."

"She said she'd take the best boy off the train," someone else shouted. "So we all brought our boys."

"She doesn't have any money."

Brianna's heart sank at Trey's words. What was he doing?

"We seen it," Melvin said. "That there satchel is full of money."

Trey held out his hand. "Give me the satchel."

Brianna clung to the bag. She felt her whole life

174   *Nancy J. Parra*

falling apart like a sandcastle in the tide. Her panicked thoughts told her she was being betrayed yet again.

"Brianna," he said. "Give me the bag." His eyes told her to trust him. Her heart told her to trust him. She just had so much to lose if he betrayed her.

She glanced at her little brother. His eyes were wide with fear.

"Brianna."

Trey's face was not stern but demanding. She had to make a leap of faith, follow her heart, and trust him. She handed him the bag.

"Thank you." He said the words simply, but they held a wealth of meaning.

He opened the bag and pulled out the money she did have. Then he dumped the paper bundles at his feet. The crowd roared its anger, and terror burned through her, leaving a bitter taste in her mouth. He was betraying her after all. She took a step back and shielded Ethan with her body.

Trey silenced the room with a wave. "She does not have money, but I do, and you all know it."

There was murmuring.

"I will reimburse every man here two hundred for his boy. That's all you're going to get. So you can take it or leave it."

"Two hundred dollars!" Zeke blustered. "I ain't giving up the boy for no two hundred dollars."

"I'm afraid you have to," said another voice from the back of the room.

Bri took another step back, her heart pounding, her

brain working fast. Trey had told the sheriff. She clutched her brother's hand in anticipation of flight.

Jeb stood in the back of the room with his arms crossed and a stern look on his face. "You either take the money as a reimbursement for your losses or I'll have to arrest every man here for slave tradin'."

Bri could not believe her ears. The sheriff was going along with Trey.

"Gentlemen," Trey said. "Form a line to the right. Once you get your money, I don't want to see or hear of you ever adopting another child. Jeb will be sure and tell me if you do."

"That's right. Just by being here, you all have forfeited your rights. Now line up." Jeb caught her eye and winked.

Brianna let out a sigh of relief. Her heart pounded hard in her ears, but it was going to be all right. She pulled Ethan in beside her. "It's going to be okay," she said.

The other boys looked at her. She smiled at them. "Its okay. Mr. Morgan is a good man."

"Are you going to adopt us?" little Jeremy asked.

Speechless, she glanced at Trey. He pulled money out of a pouch and handed it to the last miner.

"Ma'am?" The boys were gathered around her. "Are you going to adopt us? Or do we have to go back to the Westside Lodging Home for Homeless Boys?"

They held their hats in their hands, and the sight of them broke her heart.

"Please," Jeremy said. "Please don't make me go back there." He reached out and took her free hand.

"Don't you worry," she said. "I'm going to adopt you. I'm going to adopt you all."

"Yes, *we* are," Trey answered. He broke through the crowd of boys and stepped in to take Brianna's hand.

"We are?" she asked.

"Yes," Trey said firmly. "Now you boys gather up your stuff. We have a train to catch."

"Where're we going?" Mick asked.

"Wyoming," Trey said. "I own a large ranch. There will be plenty of room for everyone."

"Do we have to work in a mine?"

"The only work you'll be doing is going to school. And helping out around the ranch of course. That's what families do. They help each other."

"Bri?" Ethan asked.

"It's okay, Eth, get your things." She turned to Trey with her heart in her eyes. "Thank you. But you don't have to do this. Really, I know how you feel about family. The boys and I will be all right."

"You trusted me," he said. "Last night you trusted me with the truth. This morning you trusted me to help."

"I realized that I loved you. If I loved you, I had to trust you."

He reached down and grabbed her, pulling her off her feet and planting a huge kiss on her mouth before he set her down.

"Then trust me with one more thing. Come home with me."

"Home?"

"Marry me, Bri. I want nothing more than you and

my boys to come live in my house and make it a home. I've realized how wrong I was. I want to be part of a family."

"Do you love her?" Ethan asked.

"I love her," Trey told him. He turned to Brianna. "I think I fell for you the moment you said you wanted me, dead or alive."

The heat of a blush rose over her cheeks and happiness filled her heart. "I want you all right, Trey Morgan. I knew it from the moment I first saw your picture on that poster."

"Handsome devil, aren't I?"

She held him close. "I crossed the wilderness to find you."

"Smart woman," he said and turned to Ethan. "Smart women are the best to have around. Let's go home."

Epilogue

Brianna McGraw looked down the aisle and had the sudden realization that every person in the small town of Amesville had stuffed themselves into the church.

Her heart leapt into her throat and threatened to leap right out of her mouth. She struggled to take a deep breath.

Trey took a hold of her hand and squeezed it. She looked up into his handsome notorious face and smiled. It had only been three days since they arrived, and already this town had claimed them as their own.

The boys had spent the time getting used to their new accommodations and grumbling about having to go to school. Brianna glanced at them. All fifteen boys had asked to stand in the front of the church. The preacher had obliged. She realized that she was surrounded by men.

Instead of bridesmaids, she had sons. Trey had his brothers as his best men. The Morgan men were all tall and intimidating, but they accepted her on sight. It was a strange experience. Bri was used to relying only on herself. Now she not only had Trey, but she had his two brothers as well. She couldn't have asked for better for her brother or the other boys.

"You may now kiss the bride," the preacher droned.

Trey pulled Brianna toward him. She smiled at the sheer happiness she saw in his eyes. "I love you," she whispered.

"I know," he replied and kissed her until her knees gave way. Then he picked her up in his arms and carried her through the packed church.

Brianna blushed. "Trey, put me down. What are all these people going to think?"

"They're going to think I'm kidnapping my wife."

"What?"

"Throw your bouquet, darlin', we are out of here."

"But—"

"Toss it while you can," he ordered as they approached the church door.

If there was one thing she had learned through all this, it was that Trey was a man of his word. She tossed the bouquet over his head and into the scrambling crowd.

A cheer went up. Brianna peeked over Trey's shoulder to see who caught it. It was Taggart Morgan. The big man frowned and tossed the bouquet aside and pushed after them.

"What are you grinning about?" Trey asked as he tucked her into a waiting carriage.

"Taggart caught the bouquet."

Trey chuckled as he jumped up. "Matt told me Tag would be next." He snapped the reins and started them off at a breakneck pace.

Bri grabbed her hat with one hand and the seat with her other. "We can't just leave," she shouted. "What about the party?"

He glanced at her. "They'll be fine without us."

She looked behind her and saw the brothers mounting their horses. "Well, if you want to lose them you'd better hurry."

"Don't worry, darlin', I have a plan."

Indeed he did. It was a plan worthy of Brianna Mc-Graw. In less than two hours, they had hidden the carriage and taken waiting horses up into the mountains. Brianna was proud to watch Trey's backtracking skills and they were soon very much alone.

"Where are we going?" she finally asked.

They crossed the top of a ridge and a small valley lay spread beneath them. At the base of the valley, a stream trickled, and beside the stream was a cozy cottage. Smoke curled up through the chimney.

"This is my parent's first cabin," Trey said. "I come here sometimes to be alone."

Brianna sighed. *Alone* sounded like such a nice word. Since they had rescued the boys they hadn't had a moment alone. "I like that word," she said as they approached the cabin.

"Yeah," he said and glanced at her sideways. "Me, too."

They stopped the horses in front of the porch and Trey helped her down. "Come on," he said and took her by the hand. "I have a surprise for you."

She followed him to the door.

"Wait."

"What is it?"

He grabbed her and picked her up. "Tradition." He carried her across the threshold. "Welcome home, Mrs. Morgan."

Brianna's eyes widened. The cabin was a single room with a small wood-burning stove; two horsehair stuffed chairs, a small tea table, and a very large bed. But the furniture wasn't what caught her attention. What made Brianna gasp was the walls. They were covered with bookshelves filled from floor to ceiling with books.

"Trey?"

"I didn't want you to get homesick for your library," he said. "So Matt, Tag, and I came up with this idea." He set her down. "We thought, what with so many boys and all, you might need a place of your own on occasion. So, this cabin is my wedding gift to you."

Tears welled up in Brianna's eyes. "I don't know what to say."

Trey drew her close. "Tell me you like it."

"I love it!"

"Good," he said and planted a kiss on her forehead. "I love you, Brianna Morgan."

"I love you too." Brianna reached up and wound her arms around Trey's neck and kissed him until his knees were weak and there was nothing left for them to do but fall back on that big, beautiful bed.